DEBORAH LAMOREAUX

Verndari Awakening
Father, Creator, Spirit -
by
Deborah Lamoreaux

ISBN: 978-1-965352-99-1

PROLOGUE

"Thank you for agreeing to sit outside."

She took in the scene around the outdoor café. Looked out at her spectacular view of the Mediterranean Sea. La Belle Côte d'Azur – the beautiful blue coast. "Nice is so beautiful this time of year. Isn't it?"

She glanced over, just as he nodded. Gave her that attractive half smile of his.

She took a deep breath in, closed her eyes for just a second as she smelled the salt in the air, and enjoyed the warmth of the sun on her skin. She turned, watched the people strolling along the boardwalk, in the bright sunshine.

"Où vas-tu?! Où vas-tu?!" A young father in the nearby square called out, enquiring about a toddler's planned destination, as he raced after him. She grinned as she heard the child's joyful giggles, then shook her head as she watched him try to make good his futile escape.

"Children sure are surprisingly quick at that age, aren't they?"

"Oh, they're a joyful handful all right."

To his credit, the kid managed to get a few meters away, at least, before being scooped up and tickled to his shrieking pleasure, when his father finally caught up with him.

"So, I met you here to let you know Senator Finn Berring is definitely your guy."

"I'm sorry, who?" She turned back. Looked across the table.

"Senator Berring? You should arrange a meeting with him. I've been told he's trying to set himself apart. Genuinely supporting his constituents, instead of serving his own interests. He doesn't want to be seen as just another useless piece in a broken system. So, he'll be sympathetic to your cause."

"Really? That's good to know. We've been knocking on so many doors and getting them all slammed in our faces of late. I like to think of myself as the optimist in our group, but I'm telling you, even *I* have been losing hope. You think he'd really be open to helping us get the funding we need?"

"I do."

"Well, okay then. I'll reach out to his team as soon as possible."

"Good."

She nodded, then looked down, only just noticing the delectable assortment of pastries on her plate, artfully adorned and filled with fresh cream, fragrant chocolate, and fruit. Alarmed, yet at the same time delighted by the sheer size of what she could only describe as a 'died and gone to heaven' selection. She took a moment to savor the sight and the sweet aromas.

She would have dug in with relish too… *IF,* she'd been alone.

Wondering if he'd noticed, and thought her 'healthy' appetite a deal-breaker, she pushed it slightly aside. Took a delicate sip from her teacup instead, then set it down and smiled at him.

"What's the matter? Not hungry?"

"Huh?"

"I happen to know those are all your favorites. Go ahead…dig in."

"Oh, I'll probably just pack them up in a doggy bag to go. You know us girls, have to watch those calories." She beamed at him.

He eyed her. His left brow lifted nearly to his hairline.

"Now that's a shame. I was so looking forward to seeing the expression on your face as you enjoyed them."

He shrugged, even as a slight smile graced his handsome features. "Suit yourself."

Well, wasn't that refreshing!

A man who would tolerate, let alone enjoy, watching a woman consume this much dessert was a rarity for real. This one must be special.

Plus, it was strange. She'd only just met him, but he seemed so familiar somehow. Like that person you keep seeing everywhere, even talk to every now and again, but never for long cnough to actually gel to know them. Maybe this was just the perfect opportunity to change that.

She smiled back. Put out her hand, inviting him to shake it.

"By the way, I'm–"

"No. No names this time."

"Excuse me?"

He leaned in, lowered his voice as his gaze became intense. Penetrating.

"They're coming. They'll be able to track you. Find out who you are."

"What? Who? What are you talking about?"

She tried to follow what he was saying. Looked into his eyes. Intense, bright blue held her gaze. Captured her mind. He raised an index finger. Held it up about six inches from her face. Mesmerized, she followed it. Watched as he moved it slowly left, then right, then forward.

He tapped her forehead.

She flinched. Heard the sound of her sharp intake of breath as she sat up in bed, and in the dark.

"Now, just *what*…in the great beyond, was that?"

Chapter 1

Ecclesiastes 4:10
For if they fall, the one will lift up his fellow...

Elise looked around the darkened room.

Still seeing and feeling the lingering impact of deep, penetrating, bright blue eyes, her brain registered the dim moonlight filtering in through partly open glass doors, leading out onto a balcony.

She pulled back the covers. Swung her legs over and set her feet down.

In something cold…and fluid.

"What in the world?"

She looked down. There was water. Everywhere. She lifted one soaked foot and then the other. Unable to believe what she was seeing, and then hearing, as a horrific roaring sound jarred her already edgy nerves. Tugging her gaze to the glass doors and the ocean visible beyond them.

Oh, dear God…

Dark. Turbulent. Monstrous. A tidal wave. The size of a mountain. Churning high above the dimly moonlit horizon. Headed her way and moving in fast, and that could mean only one thing…

She was in the void.

Again.

That place. Between sleep and waking.

Mesmerized, unable to move, or even look away, she watched as the enormous tsunami crashed onto the rocky beach, a fair distance beyond the room.

And then climbed, as the sheer power of the water consumed everything in its path as it pushed onward.

Like a living thing, the foamy wave rolled upward from the beach, and surged between and over the balcony railings. The glass doors burst open then, as water began rushing into the room.

Regaining her will to move she wasted no more time and leapt, straight up to the ceiling. And a moment before her head hit it, she turned, pressed her back against it instead. Scooted backward and crouched in a damp corner as she watched the water's swift rise. One second more, then two, before she squeezed her eyes shut, took a deep breath, and propelled herself upward through the moss-covered ceiling, and into the room above. Wondering all the while if whatever she was about to encounter there, would be even worse.

Her head, shoulders, waist, then her thighs cleared the floor. She felt the water below tug on her ankles. She pulled her knees up, felt her bare toes scrape across the ice-cold floor, a scant second before she was yanked sharply backwards. She gasped, kept her eyes tightly closed as she felt her arms jerk forward with the force of the change in direction. They dropped to her sides again, a few moments later as she reversed course and was pulled along towards whatever was ahead, but thankfully at a smoother and less harrowing pace. And just as she began to hear, or rather feel, a persistent clamor.

Deep and unmistakable it called to her. Overshadowing her body's trembling and the echo of her harsh, erratic breaths. Consuming her every thought, until she knew she just had to get to it.

A few moments passed. Then a few more. Then she slowed. Calmed down. She opened her eyes a crack to take a look at her surroundings.

There.

She saw just a flash of something unusual at the very center of the crush of pressing souls some distance away and below her.

This must be the same person she'd been feeling so compelled to help of late. She'd ignored all the other times she felt the gentle whisper. Out of fear and disinterest. But this time was different. The tugging sensation felt urgent in her spirit. Strong. Continuous and far more insistent. She didn't even know how, but once she'd made her decision to submit to the feeling, she'd felt buoyed, lighter, and carried along to her current destination.

A large multi-ceilinged room.

Trying to think of the best way to get to the exact location without being noticed, she flew above and between the different sections until she was floating, just over the spot. Behind a large, circular, low hanging panel. Low enough to reach her target. Hoping for some kind of divine camouflage, to obscure their view of her, at least for a little while, as carefully as she could, she leaned down, and dipped her hand into the fray. Cringed as she felt their cloying cold.

"Here! Take my hand. Quickly!" Hoping the object of her rescue effort would sense and understand her, she wiggled her fingers around a bit, as much and for as long as she dared, or could stomach, then pulled back. Suppressed a deep shudder as she tried to forget just how icky it had felt

as her hand speared through their clammy bodies.

In the next instant a hand appeared just above the gelatinous sea, and she grasped it. Feeling its tell-tale warmth, confirming it was indeed a living, breathing, transcended soul like her. She gathered a burst of speed, and pulled. Shot upward. And didn't look back.

Up through the many ceilings of that room, and then the floor above, she flew. Through levels upon levels of never-ending confined spaces, glimpsing things she'd never seen and hoped to never, *ever*, see again. Until – there it was. On the left. Just a sliver of sunlight, peeping in through a miniature window in one of the largest areas she'd seen in a very, very long while.

She slowed her ascent halfway through the floor and looked around.

Walls, ceiling, floor. All of it. Entirely made of wood. Unmistakable also given the pungent smell of fresh varnish assaulting her senses, and emanating from all around her. Mostly she guessed, from the hundreds of open tins and paint brushes, lined up neatly against the far wall. Still, it was blessedly devoid of lost souls, so despite the smell, she counted her lucky stars she was alone. Completing her rise through the floor, she turned in midair and prepared to fly straight at the tiny window.

"Whoa there! Are you crazy?! We won't fit through there. What are you thinking?"

A voice – masculine, deep, ragged, and distressed, echoed somewhere in the back of her mind. Reminding her she actually wasn't alone. And as if to reinforce that fact, the already firm grip he had on her hand tightened, even as a sudden, weighty drag forced her to a complete halt, and then down to the floor.

On her tiptoes, she looked down. Absorbed the intense sensation of tacky but solid wood beneath the balls of her feet. Lifting off a couple inches, she visualized her bare feet free of the paint's stickiness and in an instant, they were back to normal. She flexed then relaxed them and rotated slowly. Mildly surprised, at just how close he was to her, and even more so that she still had to tilt her head back to look into his face.

She gazed up. Into nervous gray eyes. Shifting left. Right. Then back again, as they searched hers. And at features that though indistinct, were really quite attractive. Although, the unkempt blond hair left something to be desired. But given whatever unimaginable indignity he'd just suffered, she supposed it was to be expected. Hell, she was probably an un-coiffed mess herself by now. Who was to say? And that was only provided she actually even looked like her, on this occasion.

"So… you realize we just went through like literally hundreds of floors and ceilings, right?"

"Floors and ceilings?" He sounded alarmed.

"Uh…yeah. Didn't you notice? How could you possibly miss that?"

"Well, after I grabbed your hand, I…uh…sort of had my eyes closed…uh…until now."

He paused. Looked down at his feet, lifted one gummy looking sole then the other. Then craned his neck and gazed up at the intricately carved antique wooden ceiling high above their heads.

Plop.

He jerked, as a drop of wet varnish landed on his cheek.

Stifling an unexpected urge to giggle given his discomfited look, and…well…the fact that the circumstances in which they'd found themselves were hardly funny, she set her face to stoic instead as he looked down at her again.

"So, look around you now. I'd say we're currently standing in the varnish emporium from hell. Wouldn't you? And what? You're worried about fitting through a little ol' window, right now?"

"Okay. So, that's a fair point. I'll give you that." He reached up with his free hand and wiped at the drop on his face. Looked down, as he rubbed his thumb and forefinger together. *"How'd you do that, by the way?"*

"Do what?"

"Fix your feet. They were covered in wet paint, just like mine are. Then they weren't. True, everything's kinda blurry, but I saw them. How'd you get them clean again?"

"I dunno. Sometimes I can uh…change things. Can't you?"

He closed his eyes and got still for a couple seconds. Like he was concentrating really hard. He opened his eyes again and looked down. His feet looked the same.

"Obviously not."

"Hmm… What I do only works on me though. Or things connected to me. I can't do anything about that," she waved a hand at his feet, *"or this."* She pointed up towards the ceiling. Made a sweeping

circle with her finger.

"What is all this?"

"Tough to say. If I had to guess…some kind of purgatory maybe? A place of manifested regret, for sure."

"Yeah…I see that." He looked around. *"More like magnified, I'd say. So, I take it you've been here…done this before?"*

"A lot. And for sure, more times than I'd ever care to admit. So, don't worry, I've got you." She squeezed the hand she still held in reassurance. *"Okay?"*

"Okay." He nodded.

"Just try to relax." She looked over at the window. *"This may feel…a little strange."*

"What? You mean worse than what we've already experienced?"

"Could be. What can I say, getting out like this… I'm not gonna lie to you. It's a doggone crap shoot."

She turned, gathered her momentum, but then spun back to him when she felt his slight, but insistent tug on her hand.

"Look… whatever happens. I just wanna say… Thank you… Seriously. I don't know what I would have done…what would have happened to me, if it hadn't been for you."

Touched by the look on his fuzzy features she knew conquering her own fears had all been worth it. Just for that one look.

"Sure. Don't mention it." She smiled.

His eyes widened. His next inhalation – Sharp.

His gaze lifted. From her lips to her eyes… Dropped. Rose again…and held.

A little unnerved, she ended the moment. Turned away. Focused on her objective, and flew them straight at the tiny window at high velocity. It bulged outward with a fair amount of resistance, but then snapped back, allowing them to break through. Allowing them a blessed escape, and she hoped, their freedom from the void entirely.

Feeling more at ease, she breathed in deeply and propelled them along at a slower pace then, and on towards the growing light on the horizon in the surrounding dark night sky.

"Wow, this is so beautiful." For the first time he floated forward, looked around as he came in line and glided alongside her.

"Yeah, I guess it can be. Sometimes." She took a moment to enjoy the unique pleasure of the cool breeze blowing against her skin, and then relaxed as they were carried along side by side in silence. On angels' wings, she fancied with a smile.

"Okay, get ready." She glanced over at him.

"For what now?"

She saw the sudden blinding flash of light and gasped as she was jolted awake.

"For that."

Shaking her head on a chuckle, she wondered who he was, and what he'd be like in real life, as she rose and prepared for the day ahead.

Chapter 2

Luke 6:38
Give, and it shall be given unto you; good measure,
pressed down, and shaken together, and running over...

"Mr. B? Ms. Elise Sharpe is here to see you… Okay. Sure. Ms. Sharpe? If you'll please follow me?"

Elise had heard very little and seen even less about Senator Finn Berring in the mainstream media she followed. Wondering what he'd be like in real life, she walked in step with his executive assistant as she led her across a shiny porcelain floor to his office.

"He's just finishing up a call, so you can go right on in."

"Thank you…uh… Gretchen?" She read the glowing nametag set into the young woman's lapel. "And may I say, that outfit, it's just lovely, by the way. Too cute!" She thought she looked a little sad, and decided to share a few kind words to cheer her.

"Why, thank you. You really think so?"

"Oh yes, definitely. It's perfect for your complexion and figure and really makes the green flecks in your eyes pop too."

"OMG. That's exactly what I thought too when I bought it. But I just figured I was being silly. That no one would even notice. Thank you, so much!" The young lady beamed as she ushered her into the senator's ginormous corner office. "I love your hair, by the way. Too few ladies go for that straight, wispy, pixie cut these days. It really suits you."

"Thank you. That's so nice of you to say." She ran her fingertips through her bangs.

"Can I get you a latte, or cappuccino, or something? Or how about a snack? I think we still have some brownies left in the breakroom."

"Oh no, I'm fine, but thanks so much for offering."

"Sure. Enjoy the rest of your day."

"Thanks. You too."

Gretchen walked out with a little spring in her step that wasn't there before, and let the door swish closed behind her.

Taking in a deep breath, Elise looked around her.

The space felt cold. And she wasn't just talking about the arctic cooling system, and the floor-to-ceiling winter snowscape he had going on. The sparse furnishings, in fact the entire décor just screamed - "Don't just stand there, girl! Get the hell out! And don't even think about us validating your parking." So much so, that her very least favorite 'I' words of all time popped into her mind – Isolating. Impersonal. And… Intimidating.

Maybe this was a mistake.

She fingered the pendant on the chain at her throat. A cherished memento. A wedding band that had never managed to take its rightful place on her ring finger. She felt a certain comfort as she touched the partly sleek, partly diamond encrusted surface, and hoped for just a little of the calm, poise under pressure, and wisdom of the one who'd bought it.

She'd awoke the previous morning with such a strong compulsion to set this meeting. And with a vague recollection of why – flawless, bronzed skin. A gorgeous face, and long wavy sun-bleached locks, reminiscent of 21st century heartthrob Jason Momoa. Mmm…and mesmerizing blue eyes…

And a trip to France?

She shook her head. Clearly her lifelong desire to tour the French Riviera, among other places in Europe, was so consuming it had begun invading her dreams. Well, that and her obsession with romance novels. If her ooo-la-la… 'outdoor café in Nice' crush wasn't a figment of her very best romantic fantasies, then she didn't know what was. One day soon she'd turn those fantasies into reality. She always got whatever she set her mind to.

Case in point. She'd taken her time with her make-up that morning. Chosen just the right outfit she knew would boost her confidence, which would assure her the win. Because, make no mistake, she'd made up her mind, she wasn't leaving without it.

Of course that was her thinking up until about five minutes ago.

Now? Well…so much for that. All the internal pep talks weren't helping her even a little bit. Now, instead of time spent in personal grooming and wardrobe changes, she wished she'd used that time to google the heck out of him like a normal person would have, and like her best friend Chaz had told her to do the night before.

He'd researched and learned quite a bit about the senator. Said he was the youngest sitting member of the upper house at just thirty-two. Four years older than she was right then. He was brilliant, but an arrogant, self-centered climber, so she should resort to pandering to his ego if she felt like he wasn't swayed by her pitch. Other than that, she didn't know a dang thing about the man, or his agenda. What if he asked her if she'd voted for him?

Oh, dear God…

Maybe she could make a little joke, laugh it off somehow, when she informed him, she'd actually voted for the other guy.

Feeling awkward and nervous all of a sudden, she didn't venture in any further, but stood near to the door, but not so close that it would keep swishing open and closed behind her. Just in case she changed her mind and decided to bolt, she reasoned.

Or in case she didn't even get to stay for the duration of the thirty-minute time slot she'd been allotted. Judging from his actions just then.

Was he skiing?

She guessed she wouldn't be there much longer if he couldn't even get off the slopes for the time it took to give his 2.30 his full attention.

"Just give me one more minute. Will you, Ms. Sharpe?" He raised his left hand and lifted a forefinger. His back all but turned to her as he gestured, he resumed his conversation with whoever he was speaking to, as he faced one of his immense, immersive, and snowy glass walls. At least six foot four, he was lean, muscled, and dressed to impress in leg-hugging slacks and a soft white shirt, with a dark paisley waistcoat that stretched to screaming across his broad back and shoulders.

Wow…

And very toned triceps, she noticed, as he reached the same hand back and grabbed the jacket hanging over a new-age looking ergonomic chair.

"Okay, okay. I heard you. Now I've gotta go. My three o'clock is here." He put his arms through and shrugged into it. "You'll have my decision by tomorrow, gentlemen. Yes. Fine. Bye." Trendy patched elbows in the same pattern as his waistcoat peeped out as he buttoned it.

"I'm so sorry about that." He tapped the coin-sized communication disc at his temple and the green flashing light went off. "Now, Ms. Sharpe, what can I do to assist–" he turned around, "–you…"

It was him.

Her sometime after daybreak rescue from the night before last.

In the flesh.

He turned pale. Looked at her like he'd just seen a ghost.

"Oh wow…I can't believe it…it's really you."

Even though his previously blurry features were now at their crystal clear, and handsome best; she still recognized him. Could see that it was unmistakably him. He sounded different though. But maybe that was just because this time the deep, rich, warm tone of his voice echoed pleasantly around the room, filling that space, instead of just the one inside her head.

"Senator Berring… Well dang…this is certainly unexpected, isn't it?"

She hadn't meant to sound glib, but the words were already out there. No taking them back now.

"I'll say… Please, come on in. Have a seat."

She moved forward. As did he. Extended her hand and smiled, as they met in the center of the room. Watched his gray eyes widen, and the tone of his skin change with a slight blush as he shook it.

And held on.

For just a few moments longer than she would have considered appropriate, given the professional nature of their current meeting.

Extracting her fingers as gently as she could, she continued passed him; sank into the chair he'd indicated on her left and in front of his desk. Looked back and then followed his progress as he slowly strode around to sit behind it. Never once taking his gaze off her.

"So, you're real." He ran the fingers of both hands through his hair.

"Yes. Yes, I am. Or, at least I was, last time I checked my pulse on the VR running track at my gym." She smiled.

"Wow, you're…I mean this…this is just so amazing."

Of course, she didn't know him personally, but he seemed very pleasantly surprised. Delighted even. Like a child getting exactly what they'd asked for on their birthday, or under the tree at Christmas.

Amused, she wondered what exactly was going through his mind just then.

"I'm sorry. I must seem like a kid at Christmas, right now." He chuckled. "It's just so great to see you. The real you, I mean." He shook his head, then ran his hands through his hair again. Making it look exactly as it had the night before. Like a toddler. Adorable. Only, really, really hot.

So…sexy-cute-messy was a look for him.

Obviously.

"What?"

"Oh, it's nothing." She tried to hide a burst of a giggle behind a hand. Then relented to his inquiring look and pointed. "It's just your hair, it's… uh…" She pointed again.

"A disaster. Right? It's okay. You can say it. I know." He chuckled and shrugged. Ran a hand over it again, without any improvement. "I envy you. Yours looks amazing short, by the way. I can't seem to keep mine neat when it's this length. And I can't handle all those gels, and sprays, and goop they use to tame it whenever I have a press-op. Can't stand the way it feels."

"Yeah, I know what you mean. I don't use those products either."

"Right? I would never use that stuff every day. My hair's better when it's long. Not like a girl, or anything," he ran a hand along his neatly bearded jawline, "but longer than this. Think it looks better that way too. Of course, my administration-mandated stylist says that length isn't right for what she calls the 'Senate-ready optics'."

"Ahh… I see. So, what are we talking here? Like

Brad Pit in *Troy*, or Chris Hemsworth Marvel Universe's, *Thor* – the god of thunder, long?"

"Oh, the god of thunder. Definitely." He grinned.

"Really? Well yeah, then I can see why your stylist wouldn't go for that."

"Yeah."

They shared a smile.

"So, I know you're a busy man, and I don't want to take up too much of your time. Why I asked to meet with you is to…uh…I'm sorry, but would you mind, could you just switch off the winter-scape for a bit?" She stifled a very real shiver as she watched the condensation puff out of her mouth with every word and breath.

"Oh, of course. I'm so sorry. I forgot I had it on. I love this temp."

"I do as well. It's just I'm really not dressed for it, and I feel like I'm about to get frostbite, or something. Now if this was Christmastime?"

"In Aspen?"

"You know it." She grinned.

"Oh, yeah…there's nothing like it. The frostier the better. Am I right? Okay…let's see here…" He tapped a panel on the left side of his desk a couple times, and suddenly it was a bright, sunny day at the beach. Complete with a refreshing sea breeze, the smell of the ocean, and the faint rustling of palm fronds in the distance. Where she could just make out the gentle, foamy swells rolling up onto the sand that also suddenly appeared right beneath her favorite pair of red-bottom heels.

"Is that better?"

"Okay…first off… Wow. A girl could get whiplash from that scene-switch, but thank you. As long as this isn't the version where you get splashed with real seawater, as the tidal wave rolls in. I think I'm good. Not my idea of a fun time, by the way. Long story."

"I'll bet," he chuckled. "Well, rest easy. No chance of that. This is the professional, meeting in the workplace-friendly, visuals and atmospherics only, package. It's supposed to set people at ease and encourage open dialogue."

"Ah, so you attend a lot of *professional meetings* on the slopes, do you?"

He eyed her. "Not usually. No."

The side of his mouth twitched up in a half smile.

"As it happens, when you walked in, I was practicing a couple new edging and pressure control techniques, while I was on my conference call. It helps me sharpen my span of attention."

"What skiing?"

"No. Multitasking. It's a learned skill. With practice I find it's allowed me to really zero in on the areas of focus that are most important," his lingering gaze touched her everywhere not concealed by her side of his desk, "while at the same time still giving at least satisfactory, if not optimum, attention to others."

"Really? Well, you must be a real whiz at Minecraft parties, huh Senator?"

"Mmm…among other things."

She eyed him. "Uh-huh…"

Warning! Detour! Train derailed and off the

tracks up ahead. Proceed with extreme caution.

She couldn't be sure, but something told her he wasn't just talking about his work ethic anymore. Was he hitting on her right now? Nervous and figuring they were venturing into potentially dangerous territory, she changed direction to get them back on course.

"So, anyway, like I said, I'm trying to raise awareness for my organization and hopefully some more funding. We run homeless shelters and so much more. We're called 'Food for Thought.' So, essentially, we get people to drop off cooked meals, grocery items, toiletries, and stuff like that, in exchange for content. You'd be surprised how many people either can't schedule the time, or else are just completely incapable of coming up with something engaging, or funny, or even relevant, for their posts and reels on social media."

"Well, speaking as someone guilty of all the above, I'd have to say I'm pretty sure I wouldn't. Be surprised, that is."

"Oh, no way. I don't believe that. Not for a second. I think I've…uh…seen some of your stuff and–"

"Liar. No, you haven't."

He gave her a look. Like he'd just bared her soul and still liked what he saw.

A lot.

It should have sounded like an accusation, but instead, she just heard a call to engage, on a-whole-nother level.

"Okay, so maybe I haven't," she smiled, feeling a return of her nerves. "But if I did, I'm sure I'd enjoy it."

"That's kind of you to say, but I'm afraid self-promotion isn't my strong suit. My content sucks meteors."

"Sucks meteors? Really?"

"Okay, so that was really bad. I know, right?" He barked out a laugh and kept on laughing. It was rich and real. Filled the space in his office…and in her soul. "Don't even know why I said that. Seemed like a good idea, right up until the words were actually out of my mouth."

She smiled. "Don't sweat it. Happens to the best of us. Can't tell you the number of times I've had something slip out of my mouth that I just wanted to suck right back in there."

Oh, no…

Like maybe right now, yuh mean?! Inside her head, her mind was literally screaming at her.

His eyes had widened a fraction as soon as she said it. Even as his nostrils flared a bit, on a sharp inhalation. Plus, that very slight reddening of his face was back.

Oh, Crap…!!! Are you kidding me?! You did not just say that!

Forget being derailed. The train had just gone airborne and was on a collision course with a commercial jetliner.

"So anyway–" mortified, she felt her own face heating up and rushed to silence her inner self-censure by finishing her pitch, "–we distribute everything we collect, along with our own contributions, to the less fortunate. Many of them homeless. As you know, AI has evolved to where the majority of the only really sustainable jobs available for humans are in healthcare, education, or financial management. Or in the artistic fields like content creation, or in leadership or governance roles like yours. Millions have been laid off. And now, since the defenders made their chip tech mandatory for people wanting to access their free food dispensers, things are becoming increasingly difficult for those who've declined to get implanted.

"The defenders haven't let anyone get footage of it, but I understand it's quite a painful experience, and it leaves an odd mark. Like being branded. Once the tech they press through the skin's surface sets itself up underneath."

"Yes, I've heard. If it were up to me, I'd see that crap banned. It's barbaric." She saw the raw anger flash across his features and wondered if he was being genuine.

"You'll get no argument from me there. For some unemployed folks it was like a death sentence when they enforced that new regulation. Having their only means of accessing a meal for themselves and their kids taken away because they wouldn't comply."

Since the sitting president had pronounced himself Verndari's most avid supporter, and some kind of messiah to the people at the very start of his term in office, politics, religion, business alliances, pretty much everything, had become polarized. Much as she imagined it had been like before the arrival of the defenders.

Then came the new Verndari branding, and with it leading Christian voices in the underground web were abuzz with talk of parallels to antichrist and the mark of the beast. But they were being systematically discredited in mainstream media as alien-haters and heretics, and religious zealots, prejudiced against the defenders.

"So, I'm sure you've heard the whispers," she ventured, to get his reaction. "Do you think there's any truth to all the mark of the beast conspiracy theories?"

"I dunno. It's tough to say without any real proof. I will say though, I don't believe in coincidences, and that supernatural horror show you saved me from the other night had to be a symptom of a far bigger spiritual dynamic that's at play right now. It got me to dust off my bible reader and listen to quite a few verses as soon as I woke up, and I'll tell you what, I haven't done that in years."

"I know what you mean. I don't know if it is *the* mark, but somewhere deep inside I just know it's wrong. I don't care if I wind up starving in the streets, I'd never take it. Since I started…uh…travelling. That's just what I call what happens to me at night. I rejoined a church and I've been trying to grow in my faith. I mean I'm not as far along as I'd like to be 'cause I've still got some other personal stuff I'm wrestling with, but it's like I heard someone say, thank God I'm not where I was six months ago."

"Good for you. What church do you go to? If you don't mind me asking?"

"Oh, not at all. St. Theresa's on Freemont."

"That's not far from me. Maybe I'll come by some Sunday."

"Sure. I've found the parishioners there really

warm and welcoming, and the pastor's messages are engaging, and relatable to real life. I think you'd like it."

"I just felt such a real sense of peace and comfort after I read those verses yesterday. I think I want to go deeper. I also discerned some things I really needed to see, especially since I can't shake the thought that attack was all directly linked to something I did that day. Something tells me Verndari are not what they pretend to be. In fact, I'm certain of it." The expression on his face became intense. Focused.

"Oh wow…really? What happened? What makes you say that?"

"Not really comfortable sharing it just yet."

"Oh, of course, I'm so sorry. I didn't mean to pry. You barely know me. That was way out of line."

"Oh no, no need to apologize. That's not it. I just haven't quite made sense of it myself. I feel like I have to do that first, before I can explain it to anyone else, yuh know what I mean?"

"Yes, of course. I understand completely."

Well, if there was any doubt before in her mind as to whose side he was on, there was none now because he was most definitely not with the defenders. Score one for him!

Very few members of his administration had the guts to even hint at holding a personal dissenting opinion, let alone profess one openly like he'd just done. And the ones who had done so were practically blacklisted, or outright shunned because of it. Like that nice and decent senator from New Atlantis. What was his name again?

"So, you were saying?"

"Oh, yes…so anyway, I've also brought a presentation with me." She reached less nervous fingers into her handbag to retrieve the data dot she'd prepared, "just to give you a sense of how our business operates. Uh…if you'd like to see it?"

"No need. I already know all I need to know about you. Uh…your nonprofit, I mean. My chief of staff did the research and brought me up to speed this morning."

"Really?"

"Yes."

"Okay, so what do you think? Is it something you'd be interested in supporting? I'd love to hear your opinion, or any suggestions. Plus, I'm happy to answer any questions you might have. On anything at all. I've also included the last three years of comparative financials in the presentation pack, so you'll see that everything we do is above board and fiscally responsible. We have one of the leading financial minds in the city volunteering with us. Alrissa Cole-Wright? Don't know if you've heard of her. She runs her own financial advisory firm. Does a lot of pro bono work. Very well respected in her field and uh–"

For pity's sake, take a breath woman…

She shut her mouth and compressed her lips for good measure.

He rocked back in his chair, pushed it away from the desk, a small smile gracing his features. "Big props for being so well prepared, but it's like I said, no need for all that. It's a worthy cause, no doubt. It will also line up really well with the social development plans we have on the cards right now. Your timing is actually perfect. I think it'll be a really good fit, so, my question is – how much do you need?"

"You're kidding me, right? Just like that?"

"Just like that."

"Oh, bless God. That's such wonderful news! Thank you so much. I can't even tell you how nervous I was coming in here thinking I'd need to say just the right things to convince you to even hear me out."

"No convincing necessary. Let's talk numbers."

"Well, as you would have been told, we're fairly well supported by a couple big corporations and some generous private donors, but we…uh…we need some extra help with our new start-up. We have plans. Big plans. For expansion into the Midwest with more shelters and some small in-house clinics. Just basic health care needs. No surgical units or anything major. So ballpark? We're talking like fifty million?" She winced and held her breath in case his initial willingness to help evaporated once he heard how much it would cost.

"Okay. Sure. We can definitely make this happen," he nodded.

Thrilled beyond words, she couldn't quite believe she was getting exactly what her team needed, just like that. Without negotiating or even compromising. Never in her wildest dreams had she imagined it could be this easy, that he'd be this accommodating to their cause.

"Okay?" She beamed.

"Sure. I'm in. Just have dinner with me, so we

can discuss the details."

Screeeeeeech!

In her mind she could see herself slamming on her imaginary rental car's brakes. Making the swift course correction necessary to avoid hitting that equally non-existent cow, on that quaint Irish country road she'd been envisioning recently, courtesy of her latest favorite romance read. Where was it set again? County Kerry? Killarney? Yeah, that was it.

"Uh…excuse me?"

"You heard me…" He eyed her, his voice a rich, velvety gravel, that resonated with her on a deep and visceral level.

"And where are my manners. You must be thirsty, after all this talking." He hit a button on the control panel on his desk. Pointed, as a selection of frosty plastic bottles and glasses rose up from a section of his desk to his left. "Water?"

"Uh…no…thank you."

He rolled his chair forward, lifted two bottles and a single glass off the shiny silver tray. Set the glass and one bottle within her reach and cracked open the other. He raised it to his head, took a long swallow, then placed it down on an equally frosty looking panel nearer to him. A ring rose up from the square disc, encircling the bottle in a cylindrical cooling field. Cold, foggy air rose from it in little puffs.

"I'm sorry, but *what*…did you just say?"

"I said… Have… Dinner… With…. Me." He punctuated the last two words with a quirky half smile and a rising left eyebrow.

"Okay, so now that's what I thought you said, but obviously you're confused." She shook her head as she tried to get them back on a controlled footing. Her control. "I came here for a legitimate business meeting, *Senator*. Don't think for one second that just because of what happened the other night you can–"

"I wonder, do you know, Ms. Sharpe, the budget for these sorts of things was already approved by this administration, months ago? The money is there and entirely under my purview. There. Just waiting for me to dispense…or not, at my discretion. I will not allow my name and reputation to be tarnished, in any way, so that means I actively involve myself in every project I sign off on. Consequently, I need more details from you, and because of my schedule at the moment, that means over dinner. You can check with my admin out there, she'll tell you. I'm practically booked solid for the next two months. The only reason you got in to see me at all today is because there was an extremely rare cancellation. So, dinner. With me. This week. For me to get a handle on the nuts and bolts of this undertaking, or it's a no-go. Those are my terms, Ms. Sharpe. Take them, or leave them." He opened his palms in a brief gesture. "It's entirely up to you."

"But you can't do that."

"Really?" His brow popped back up again. "Because, correct me if I'm wrong, but I think I just did."

She rose from her chair. Placed her palms flat on his desk and leaned forward. Felt the cool, precious metal of the ring on her chain bounce against her chest with every agitated breath she took. "There's a name for that, and it's called intimidation, Senator."

To his credit, he took her most cutting glare like a champ.

Then he looked down.

Eviscerated her sharpness with his heat, as his intense gray gaze lingered…before climbing…slowly, to meet hers again. He shifted a bit in his seat. Cleared his throat.

"Intimidation? Hardly. Quid pro quo at worst," he shrugged. "In fact, I say a simple negotiation, really. Sure, we could go back and forth, but why bother, when we both already know neither of us is backing down from our positions. I've simply presented you with the terms that constitute a reasonable compromise that will redound to our mutual benefit. Right away. That's all. Either way, I want to help your organization, and you have a choice to make. And like you said, I'm a busy man, Ms. Sharpe. Remember? So, what's it going to be?"

She was tempted to tell him exactly what he could do with his little negotiation then turn on her heel and leave, but the faces of each and every one of her homeless friends, and their families. And strangely…his. Blurry, but still wreathed in gratitude, stopped her.

"Just dinner?"

"Just dinner."

"Nothing else?"

He paused, looked across his desk at her. "Nothing…that you don't initiate," he shrugged.

Well, that was an odd choice of words. If there was ever a time for a phone-a-friend lifeline, this was surely it. A good lawyer friend. Because she felt like that kind of carefully crafted statement should for sure be accompanied by the fine print no one ever read, in a similarly carefully worded contract.

She sighed. And sat.

"Fine. Where and when?"

"Thursday night? Why don't I come pick you up." He touched the com unit on his desk a couple times. "What's your home address?"

"Oh, hell no. So, that's not happening. Just tell me where and what time, and I'll meet you there."

He gave a deep chuckle. Shook his head and leaned forward again. Clasped his hands together before his face, and rested his patched elbows on his desk.

"I'm afraid I can't do that."

"And why is that?"

He eyed her. For long seconds.

"Because… I haven't decided where, and how, I'm going to take you…yet."

Her tummy did a little flip.

Dang…was it just her, or was it hot in there?

Well, you're sitting in the middle of a beachscape in twenty-eight-degrees Celsius heat, genius. What do you think?

She swallowed. Resisted the urge to immediately reach for a big ol' gulp of the water he'd offered earlier, and that she'd declined to accept. Instead, she lowered her voice a few octaves, for fear it might betray her with a tell-tale squeak. "Excuse me?"

A corner of his mouth turned up.

"By hover car, or by private jet. To the city's

newest crave spot. Or, to this really fantastic little Italian restaurant I've been to in Rome."

Given the nonchalant way he discussed a dinner date that could require an international flight, she supposed for him it was an innocuous enough statement. Hell, she'd heard guys were taking their dates to the moon, or to Mars, to impress them, or just for kicks these days. But the way he'd spoken just now, about not knowing how he'd "take" her, just made it sound…well…racy…and really. Like really…

Hot.

A pox on her obsession with every steamy, alpha-male, one-liner she'd ever committed to memory… For surely that was the only reason why she'd read more into his statement than he obviously intended.

"Rome? I see…" She tapped her fingernails on his desk. "Don't like the Italian food right here in NYC, huh?"

"Didn't say that."

He hadn't *said* much of anything about this dinner plan of his.

She sighed.

He smiled.

"Okay fine. You can pick me up. But at the shelter, after work."

"Great! So, let's say, around seven? That work for you?"

"I'll be there."

She tapped a few of the colorful communications data dots stamped into a decorative circle all around her wrist, so she could send him her digits. "My personal contacts and the New York shelter's, are all in there."

"Great." He tapped the panel on his desk. "Got 'em. And these are mine."

She got an immediate alert on her coms. She opened her hand and the e-screen with his info popped up just above her palm.

"Whoa, this is really tiny. I can barely read these." She used the forefinger on her other hand to scroll up and down.

"Oh, sorry. I put a compression filter on there the last time I used the proximity transfer. Just tap that icon there, it will activate the zoom function and it will get bigger."

"Okay, I see that. Cool."

He rose and extended his hand. "A true pleasure meeting you. For the second time, Ms. Sharpe. Until Thursday."

She rose as well and shook it. "Senator." Then she turned and headed for the door.

Chapter 3

Philippians 4:6
Be careful for nothing; but in everything, by prayer and
supplication, with thanksgiving, let your requests be
made known unto God...

"You know, I have to say…I thought it would be bigger."

She tilted her head to the side… and stared at it for a couple more seconds in careful contemplation.

Then raised her gaze. Looked up and smiled. Into the same beautiful blue eyes, she remembered so well.

"Excuse me?"

"The Mona Lisa." She gestured to the painting hanging on the wall some distance away. "It always looks so impressive in photos. Yuh know? In presence and in size. I mean, not like 'The Last Supper' big, but bigger than this. I've always dreamed about visiting Paris to see it and there it is. Displayed on a huge wall. All on its own, and I cannot believe no one ever mentioned how tiny it is. Just like…what is that? Like letter sized?"

"It's thirty by twenty-one inches, to be exact."

"Really? That much? You sure? 'Cause it looks smaller. Of course, it doesn't help that we have to stand this far away. I was hoping to get within like a foot of it. Do you think that guard over there would mind? Would he react? Yuh think? Like haul off and take me down, or something? If I just hopped over this barrier to get a closer look?" She fingered the red velvet rope that was stopping them and a line of at least a hundred other people from getting too close to the world-famous painting.

"But you could take him? Right?"

She let her gaze roam free. Greedy for the sight of him, it journeyed all up and down his easily six foot six and two hundred and some pounds frame…of solid, just gorgeous, muscled perfection. Casually dressed in a chest-hugging white t-shirt and jeans.

"Aww yeah. You could definitely take him."

She licked her lips.

"Really?"

Her gaze snapped up, and her breath-stealing tour ended, at his hypnotic, amused crystal eyes, under a raised left eyebrow.

"Okay, fine. So clearly, retaliatory violence is not an optimal solution. But, come on! I mean, how could I not go for it. I'm standing here, in my fantasy Louvre, for Pete's sake! Are you kidding me?!" She let out a little shriek.

"Wait…this *is* just another dream, right?"

"Well, yes and no. It's complicated. Anyway,

we're not here just to look at art." He grasped her hand, pulled her out of the line, and led her to a quiet spot near the back of the room. Amid her protests.

"Aw, come on. Now we lost our spot in the line. Seriously?"

"Yes. Seriously. I knew how much you'd enjoy getting a look at that painting, true, but I also brought you here because I have a message for you, Elise."

"Oh, so we're using first names this time. Now that's progress." She turned to face him fully, gave him her most winning smile, stuck out her hand for him to shake, and dropped her voice a few octaves. "And you are?"

"Kaitiakimohlokomedi."

She felt an immediate joy-filled buzz as he grasped her hand. And such warmth. Emanating from somewhere around him. She couldn't explain it, but it felt like it flowed through him, into her, and then back again, in a never-ending pleasure loop. Such an absorbing feeling in fact, that she found herself at a loss when it came to wrapping her brain around the rather complex pronunciation of the name he'd just uttered.

How had her subconscious even come up with a name like that, anyway?

Like whatever happened to Larry, or Steve?

You know, something that every other self-respecting dreamer in the free world, or at least the great state of New York, would conjure up.

"I'm sorry…what-now? Could you please repeat that?"

"No worries. You can just call me Kai." That attractive half smile of his was back.

"Oh, thank God."

He shook his head, his face transforming into gorgeous, as his half smile became a full-on beam-fest.

"Okay…so, you're smiling. Plus, I know this isn't real. But somehow, I still feel like I should apologize. So here goes. That did not come out right. And I should know better because I made every single member of my staff go through an entire session of sensitivity training when we started our nonprofit. And rule number one is there is nothing so important to anyone as their name. And you, have a perfectly, lovely name. It's just I got distracted when I shook your hand, and I really don't think I could pronounce it, or maybe even remember it…uh…once I wake up. No offence."

"Absolutely none taken. But what makes you think this isn't real?"

"Well, duh?! We're standing in the Louvre. In Paris! Unless you're some kind of 'welcome to your fantasy vacation' kidnapper, I'm pretty sure this is all fake. Like me pretending I'm something I'm not, like dyeing my hair purple, kinda fake.

"See?" She reached out with her thumb and forefinger. Pinched as much skin as she could on his formidable forearm.

Oh, wow…

She didn't get a hold of very much.

"Yes, thank you. I felt that. But FYI and by the way, you're supposed to pinch yourself, not me."

"Oh right, my bad." She rubbed the spot on his arm, then let her hand travel along to the back. Somewhere above his elbow. Where she could test her grip on his equally impressive triceps.

"Couldn't resist doing that, could you?" He grinned.

"Nope." She barked out a laugh.

"Look, there are many spiritual dimensions of real, Elise. Just because it's a stretch, even for your wildest imaginings, doesn't make this fake. Besides, it's your soul. Your mind. Processing and interpreting external stimuli. That's what makes anything…everything actually… Real."

"Well, thank you, Morpheus!" She clapped her hands together three times. "I'll be sure to take the *blue* pill next time. Oh, and please, say hi to Neo and Trinity for me, by the way."

He looked at her like she'd just grown another head.

"It's a *Matrix* reference. A 20th century movie?"

"I know that. I've seen it. AND all the sequels and prequels, just as many times as you have."

"Huh?"

"Like, can we just not?" With a wave of his hand, he dismissed her query. "Seriously? I can't believe we're having this conversation right now." His voice was soft as he shook his head.

"Okay…" she blew out a breath, "So, you said you have something to say?"

He nodded.

"Well, go ahead. I'm all ears."

"Something's about to happen."

"What? In here?"

He shook his head. It tilted to the side a bit as his eyebrows raised.

"Oh…you mean out there."

He nodded. "You're going to feel like you're being tested, but you're not. You'll feel like everything you think you know about yourself and other people, is wrong. It will demand a certain response from you, *if* you are to benefit from it as intended, in the fulness of time. Which is why I'm here."

"And you know this, how?"

"I'm a messenger. A protector and a guide, if you will."

"So what? You're saying you're like, an angel…or something?"

"A guardian. Yes."

"Really? Whose?"

"Yours."

He said that single, little word, and just like that, she saw a revelation of the immense blessing he had been in her life, up to that point, in overwhelming flashes in her mind.

"Oh…wow…that was amazing."

"To God be the glory."

"I guess." She looked around, took in the scene as people strolled in and out. Still not as comfortable as she wanted to be with the mention of a supreme being who'd seen fit to take away the love of her life. Her high school sweetheart. Her very first and only crush. When he'd been in the very prime of his young life. Just starting a promising career. Killed by a drunk driver on Thanksgiving. How tragically clichéd.

Her sweet Danny.

He'd been an architect. Was growing his business and had plans to build them the most beautiful home she'd ever seen. They'd get married, move in and have a couple kids. Settle in and live life.

Instead, she'd lived his death.

Suffered through years of agonizing regrets and 'only ifs.' Very effectively punished, for some unknown reason, if that was the intent.

Kai touched her arm with gentle fingers. "He does not punish, El."

"What?" Her gaze snapped to his – tender and filled with genuine concern.

"God... He is love, grace, and mercy personified."

Most of her friends had shortened her name to Lise. No one had called her El since Danny. It was his, and only his, personal and intimate title for her.

And with that simple endearment, any doubt left in her mind that he was who he said he was, evaporated.

"He is love and truth and life. He does not punish."

"Oh, really? Well, what would you call hell then?"

"A choice."

"Excuse me?"

"The decision to choose hell, or heaven, eternal separation, or unending joy, lies with each individual. Thus, either state of being is simply an inevitable consequence, of that choice. In the midst of earthly life there is death. It is the way of the fallen world. Life is a gift. An infinite, sanctified blessing from Him who alone can sustain it."

A smile of such joy crossed his features.

Only to be replaced by one of such sadness, in the very next moment.

"You've read His Word, so I know you understand that hell was created for Legion, not for you. *Never* for you, the beloved. Yet you give such life to sin. As though it is thrust upon you, minute by minute, by some kind of evil deity. But its chief proponent, the father of lies has himself simply made a choice. *You* give him power where he has none. Dominion that cannot be taken, that is yours and yours alone to *give*. Sin for you, much like hell, is just a choice. It cannot sustain itself. It does not come from The One – the *only* source of all good and eternal things."

She was left speechless, as she let his words sink in. A revelation like she'd never experienced before took root in her mind in that very moment, changing her forever.

"Look, if it's of any comfort to you, Danny has come to great joy. You already know that. Yes?" His gaze, much like his words, pierced her soul. "He lives. A glorious eternity of connection with the Three in One."

Touched and even cheered, by the look of buoyant serenity and certainty, stamped into his attractive features and bright, beautiful eyes, she nodded. Blinked back tears, as she wasn't in the least surprised. Danny had been deeply spiritual from the time she met him, having been raised in the faith from infancy. He'd been slowly but consistently reeling her into it before he'd passed. Somewhere in her spirit she knew he wanted her to continue on the journey he'd set her on, so she was trying. Even though he wouldn't be there to walk it with her.

"Okay." She blew out a noisy breath. "So, some challenges are coming my way. Of course, the cynical side of me wants to ask how that would be different from any other day? But I won't."

"Well, except you just kind of did."

"Semantics." She waved away his words and quirky, adorable smile. "So, do I get a code word? You know, something I can think, or say, to let you know I need you and want to see you?"

"Not how this works. I'm always with you. You just didn't know it until now." He reached out and tapped her forehead with a smile. "At any rate, it's not about me. You already possess what you think you seek. In everything, by prayer and supplication, with thanksgiving, let your requests be made known unto God. It's all you need. It's all anyone needs."

"And you should know, since Danny's been gone, I'm fairly rusty where that whole prayer thing is concerned. I've been trying, but not sure I even know how to do what you just said."

"Have faith. You will. All in His good time."

"Uh-huh." She could see the confidence shining in his face and eyes and wondered if and when she would indeed share his optimism.

"Okay, and speaking of time. I need to send you back. You ready?"

She nodded, "I guess," watched as he lifted his index finger, moved it left–

"Wait!"

"What?" His finger stilled.

"Any chance we could take just a little, teeny-weeny detour back to Nice?"

"That plate of pastries is calling your name, huh?" He grinned.

"Like you wouldn't believe." She erupted into giggles.

"I knew you wanted it. And to think you had me rethinking your diet like that. Come on now."

"And now you're speaking my language because if those desserts are your version of a diet, I say, bring it on!"

"No not that kind of diet. Your Dream Implementation, Elevation, and Transformation experience."

"My dream-whaty-what-now?"

"It's essentially dream amplification. Your very best and brightest wishes. Only on steroids."

"Okay… Great! So, *now* that I know I can basically inhale that entire plate of pastries, without weight gain, or guilt, or having to give a crap about what you'd think of me. No offence."

"Again. None taken." He chuckled with her.

"Get ready Kai, 'cause I see like a ton-load of candy, and cake, and ice cream, with whipped cream and sprinkles, in my dream future. Especially if there's trouble coming."

She tried to joke about it, but inside she felt the rise of vague anxiety.

"Sure. I got you. You know that, right?" He tilted her chin up with a gentle touch. Held her gaze in his bright blue one. It turned serious, in the moment. And she just knew. He wasn't talking about supplying her with her favorite sweets.

"I'm starting to," she smiled.

"My girl!" He held out his fist, and she bumped

hers against it. "Let's do this."
He snapped his fingers.

Chapter 4

Proverbs 14:29
He that is slow to wrath is of great understanding;
but he that is hasty of spirit exalteth folly...

Snap! Snap! Snap!

"What?! What's happening?!" Startled half to death, Elise's head popped up from the report she'd been engrossed in, as she heard the sharp sound of snapping fingers at her door.

"It's 6.30, Lise. Shouldn't you be getting ready for your big date by now?"

Her best friend, work husband, and head of the nonprofit's Content Creation division, Chaz Simpson, stood in her doorway. Tall, dark, and sinfully good looking, he rotated his forefingers, signaling to her to get moving.

"Oh crap! Is it that late already?" She consulted her watch for confirmation.

"Yes. It is. And you know you don't wanna be late for your *big* date."

"Okay, yeah, thanks for the reminder." She jumped up and raced over to the rack she kept in her office for donated clothing people dropped off with her from time to time.

"And for pity's sake, will you please stop saying "big date." I told you, this is a *dinner meeting.* That's all. The senator is very busy and this is the only time he could fit me in." She reached out, to the very end of the shiny metal rod, and pulled the outfit off the hanger she'd picked out of her closet that morning.

"Uh-huh… So why do you have on those brand-new 'I'd let you do me, if I wasn't a Christian saving it for marriage' shoes, if it isn't a date? Huh?"

She tried to glare him into silence. And failed…

"And dinner? Possibly in Italy, I believe you said? Now, you know I'm all about Shelby, right?"

She nodded as he referred to his lovely wife of ten years, and one of her dearest friends in the world.

"So, don't tell her I said this, but when we started dating, it wasn't a 'love', or even an 'infatuation at first sight', kinda thing. For us it was a slow burn. So, suffice it to say, on our first date she woulda been lucky to get the Wednesday night international buffet at that upscale fast-food restaurant you like so much. Let alone an *actual* dinner overseas. Say what you like, baby-girl. Take it from a man. A man who knows how other men think. Your senator is in 'love at first sight' love, and this is a date. And not just any ol' date. This is a 'gotta impress her big-time 'cause if I blow it, I may never get this chance again', date. I'm talking 'diamond on that ring-finger, for the rest of our lives' date, two point three kids, a minivan, and a house with grass. Because I'm telling you, I gotta get, have…and hold…that–!"

Her gasp and shriek of laughter were so loud that

one, or both of them, drowned out the end of what she already knew he was about to say. "Oh really, Chaz? You are incorrigible. You did not just say that?!" A giggle erupted from her lips.

He nodded. "You better trust. This is happening, Lise. Mark my words. We are gonna laugh about this very conversation we're having, later. If I had to guess…? Somewhere between your wedding and the first of the two point three kids. Hell, why wait!" He threw his head back and roared.

And infectious as always, she couldn't help but join in. No matter how difficult a day she was having, he was always there to lift her spirits. Ready with a social media generated joke, or some colorful anecdote of his own.

And he'd been her most genuine and avid support after Danny died. He'd been there for her. Seen her through the worst of it then too.

So, it was just natural that when she floated the idea of the nonprofit three years earlier, he'd been right there with her, helping her build it from the ground up, and into the success it became. Cheering her on.

Just like always.

Like the three musketeers she, Danny, and Chaz had been inseparable from the time they'd met as children. C. D. and E. Other friends later joked that they followed each other, just like the letters in the alphabet. You saw one, just wait, the others wouldn't be far behind, they'd say and laugh.

She'd been a tomboy when she was younger. Holding her own with both boys and their friends. She could climb, fish, and play sports. Beating the pants off both of them nine times out of ten. Well, until she realized that her love for Danny was…different from her love for Chaz. Then she went through a phase of losing to him. Continually. She thought it would both boost his confidence and make her seem more girly and feminine, compared to how she'd been in the past, and he'd notice her. In the way she'd started to see him.

Of course, she didn't know it at the time, but he felt exactly the same way. Way before she did. So as soon as he picked up on her signals, and once she'd turned eighteen, he was only too eager to confess his more than brotherly love for her. Had also promptly dispelled that misnomer, set her straight about just what a turn on it was for him to behold her feminine power in all its glory. That it was one of the first things that attracted him to her in the first place. Let her know it would be his greatest pleasure to be rescued by her. Any time.

Well, she hadn't been able to rescue him that night.

That terrible night when all the feminine power in the world wouldn't have made a blind bit of difference to the tragic outcome.

7.34pm

Wondering what was keeping the senator, she tried his number again. Then, checked her messages for the fifth time. Nothing.

What if he'd been hurt, or worse. A flashback to the night she'd received the bad news about Danny played out in her mind in vivid detail.

Oh God...

The musical alert on her coms pinged.

"Hullo?"

"I'm so very sorry. I just got here. I'm outside on the street. Can you come down?"

"Yeah, I'll be there in a minute."

Oh, so he wasn't dead in a ditch somewhere, he was just late.

Really, really late.

She grabbed up her handbag, got to her office door and dearly wished for one of those antique wooden ones she'd seen a couple times that she could have slammed behind her to help vent some of her anger.

"Don't start with me Chaz! Trust me. I'm in no mood."

On her way out, just one look at his face as she stomped across the main floor, in the direction of his open office door, had her preempting whatever she already guessed he was about to say. He held his palms up and shook his head. She hung a right and headed for the exit. Caught a glimpse of herself in the entryway 3-D mirror and noticed her lipstick was all gone. Stopped with the thought to reapply it, but then–

"Yuh know what? Whatever." She snapped her purse shut and headed for the door.

"G'night Barry." She waved to the evening shift security guard as she stepped outside into the balmy evening.

"You have a good one Ms. Elise. See you tomorrow."

There he was, directly ahead at the curb, standing next to a luxury hover rental. The sleek, shiny, black kind most of the government types like him used for official business.

And a perfect match, for him.

Dressed from neck to toe in midnight black as he was. All except for the glowing red firestorm that started on the right side of the jacket, at the lapel. Like tongues of flame, they blazed an eye-catching trail, down his chest, then wound their way down, around and around a single long pant leg. Running the length of his powerful thigh and calf like the touch of a lover.

He was quite simply, stunning.

Like her own personal beacon, compelling her to come to him, in the fading evening light.

"It's really, really good to see you again." He smiled, as she approached him. His warming gaze travelled the length of her in obvious appreciation. "Again, I'm so sorry. I had a high-level security briefing I just couldn't get out of, and it went into overtime. They knocked out all our coms before we even went in, so I couldn't call you."

"And after?"

"I'm sorry?"

"After you came out of your meeting. You couldn't call?"

"In hindsight, I probably should have, but by then, I just got so focused on getting to you as quickly as possible, I just–"

"Fine. Whatever. Let's just get going."

"Hey. Hey… Come on now." He bent his head low, kept shifting his position in front of her then touched her arm with gentle fingers, so she was forced to meet his gaze and his engaging smile. "I said I was sorry. Please, don't be like that."

"Okay…fine." One really good look at that adorable head of messy hair, coupled with the warmth of his tender touch. And just like that. She managed a smile in return.

"Ahh…there she is. And bless God…that smile… I'd almost forgot how wonderful it is," he half groaned, "it could save my life. Yuh know that? I think…maybe it already did." He ran a hand down her arm to her wrist. And caught up in the heady moment, it felt only natural to her to entwine their fingers, much the same way as they'd been connected throughout their entire first encounter.

She felt the immediate and familiar sizzle between them. Took in a slow breath and stepped forward. Drawn in by his soft words, his touch, and the look in his eyes. Smoky gray… Hooded. His head lowered a fraction…her tummy did a little flip. The pleasurable sensation sending an undeniable signal to her brain that completely silenced the miniature Chaz doing the running man in her head, singing, 'I told you so. I told you so,' as she swayed closer in reckless anticipation.

For that moment, the very second when his mouth touched hers, for the very first time.

She let go of his hand, ran her hands up to his forearms. Used the leverage to tiptoe up, urged him with a look, to join her, as their lips met. And clung.

Somewhere, in the middle.

Soft. Sweet. And so very satisfying. He took her along for the single most decadent ride of her life.

Her mouth, her mind…

And the nape of her neck.

As the barest brushing of his fingers there,

against that delicate skin, set off a cascade of tingling sensation along her entire body. With a promise of more to come. A touch that communicated both comfort and hyper-awareness. Both safety…

And restrained hunger.

It was a languid, luscious, and thorough tasting, with just the right amount of pleasure and heat to keep her coming back for more. Case in point, she missed him already, as with a last nibble on her lower lip, he gently pulled back, even as she tried to follow.

He smiled. Slow and confident. Steadied her as she wobbled a bit. As he brushed a gentle thumb along the spot on her mouth he'd just abandoned, right before he released her.

"Everything I dreamed…and more," his voice came out husky as he searched her eyes. He cleared his throat.

"Huh?" Struggling for a coherent response, she basked in the afterglow of the single most impactful kiss of her young life.

"Oh, and before I forget…" He started to pull away. "Uh… You okay there?" The left side of his mouth turned up in a delightful half smile, as he steadied her yet again as she swayed towards him. Just a bit. "So, here's a little something special I got, just for you." He let go of her, waved a hand to open the hover car door, reached in, and then handed her a really large box.

"What's this?"

"A dress. Go ahead, open it. Thought it would be a nice surprise for you."

Screeeeeeech!

There it was…that pesky rental. Skidding to an

abrupt stop, in the bonny Irish countryside. Again.

"What…? Why? Because you knew you'd be late?" Alarm bells started going off in her head.

"No. I'd planned this before, actually."

She lifted the cover, even as she wondered which reason was more concerning. She read the designer labeling on the tasteful card insert, pushed a bit of the delicate tissue aside, and fingered the neckline of a luxurious red dress that could probably pay her rent for the next three months.

Like, what in the actual factual…? Are you kidding me right now? So, what I have on isn't good enough for Mr. Fancy-pants. Is that it?

"Don't you like it? I happen to know you look gorgeous in red."

"Oh. Really?! And why is that?"

"Uh… Because of what you had on. When you came to my office this week."

"Oh, right." She shook her head free of its plan to lose it. "Uh…it's lovely. Thank you."

"Don't you want to go back inside and try it on? See how it looks? I'll wait for you out here."

Suddenly uncomfortable, she looked out into the traffic on the ground and up, at the vehicles whizzing by overhead.

"Uh…no. We're already late. Shouldn't we get going?"

"Okay…" His feet shifted from left to right. He opened his mouth, then shut it again.

"Okay?" She eyed him.

"Uh, yeah. Okay…so, I guess we'll get going then."

He waved open the passenger door of the hover

car and held out his hand. She took it and he helped her in. She pushed the box the dress was in over to the corner as he got in and sat next to her. The knees of his long spread legs nearly touching hers.

The car lifted smoothly off the ground then accelerated upward.

"Can I offer you something to drink? These cars are well stocked. You can have everything from water to champagne," he pulled up a digital list off the panel on the little table in front of them. "What's your pleasure?"

"Uh, just some water, please."

"Sure, coming right up." He tapped an item on the list and two frosty tumblers of water appeared on the table.

"Here you go," he handed her one of them.

"Thank you. So…you're being surprisingly "civilian" tonight," she gestured with air quotes near her ears. "Where's your usual security detail? Thought politicians didn't travel anywhere without them these days."

"I gave my Capitol Police team the night off. It's just you, me, and my man tonight."

"Excuse me?!" She coughed, nearly choking on the sip of water she'd just taken. "Did you just say your man?"

"Oh, yeah," he chuckled, "I forgot you may not be familiar with the lingo. My mann…as in M. A. double N. It's just an acronym for Mission Android Nanite Nemesis. He's a formidable piece of nano-tech. Looks just like me. Can do everything I can, and then some, only way better. Hence the name."

"Oh, of course, I think I remember reading about

that in a press release, when they were first introduced a while ago."

"Yes, designed to provide what every modern politician needs in the ultimate portable security system. Well, that and a convenient fall guy."

"Huh?"

"Think about it. A doppelganger you can summon in the blink of an eye. He can become an energy shield. Can withstand any level of firepower. Even replicate and return it. Pretty much a weapons specialist. He's built to handle combat situations just as well as diplomacy. If it's hand-to-hand combat you need, we're talking Bruce Lee-proficient in all the martial arts, and a pugilist to rival Muhammad Ali. A certified, stone-cold, dyed-in-the-wool, one-man army that can just as easily hold his own at a negotiation table."

"So, you're saying he's not just a bodyguard? He can also switch places with you too? Essentially becoming you?"

"If the threat level calls for it. To a degree. Yeah. Or, for other reasons, like some of my colleagues, when they feel like playing hooky, and go ahead and take a couple hours off work. But you didn't hear that from me," he whispered and gave her a wink with an adorable grin.

"Oh, yeah. Of course, my lips are sealed." She returned his smile. "But aren't you worried…I mean about how the defenders could possibly use them against us?"

"Oh, no. We've put in safeguards they don't even know about. They may have had their genesis in Verndari science, but these units are completely independent and all-American. I was a part of the select committee that managed the project. We're talking brick-force level, impenetrable encryption. Certified hack-proof by our brightest tech minds."

"Wow…that's incredible."

"You have no idea. Yuh wanna see him?"

"Well, duh?! You know I do. Thought you'd never ask. Are you kidding me?"

He grinned and tapped his wrist.

An exact replica of him, even dressed the same, appeared in one of the empty seats opposite to them.

"Good evening, Senator, please state mission parameters."

"Display mode."

His digital twin leaned back, crossed a powerful leg over his knee, and then gave her one of the creepiest smiles she'd ever seen in her life.

"Okay, so can you stop him doing that, please. He's freaking me out right now."

"Yeah? Really? Okay, so this mode is kind of a work in progress. Haven't quite been able to nail it yet. I was going for something voter friendly. You know? Self-assured, but not arrogant, with just a dash of 'you can trust me with your baby?' Yes?"

She gave him an incredulous look.

"No?"

"Hell no. What *I'm* getting is 'super sketch', with a dash of 'By the way, I may just be a serial killer' thrown into the mix."

"Really? That bad? Wow. Guess I better schedule some time to iron out the kinks."

"Uh, yeah…and the sooner the better. But still phenomenally realistic though. I have to say."

"Oh, for real. And you should see his attack mode stance. I'm telling you…it's freakin' awesome!"

In her mind she could picture that really Zen-like karate pose. That beckoning hand, with the fingers positioned just so. Like when Neo was inviting Agent Smith to engage. Or that crouching down, one hand on the ground and the other arm and one leg stretched out to the side, like in every 21st century superhero movie she'd ever seen.

She witnessed the senator's child-like enthusiasm, and it was catching. "Really? Wow! Can I see it? Can I see it?"

"Well, you could, but then…"

"Don't tell me… He'd have to kill me?"

"You know it!" He barked out a laugh.

"Really?" She wanted to look exasperated with his reference to the tired action movie line, but ended up giggling instead.

"I just couldn't resist." He chuckled with her.

"I figured. It really is amazing how lifelike it is though. Seriously. Wow."

"There are subtle tells though, but you have to know what to look for."

"Hmm, Okay… I think I see what you mean. It's something in the eyes. Like there's no living, breathing soul behind them."

"Really? I can't say I ever noticed that. But you were right about the not breathing part. Look closely."

"Oh, wow. You're right. That's so obvious now that you mention it. I can't believe I didn't even notice that. His chest isn't moving. I'm such an idiot.”

“Don’t beat yourself up. Most people don’t. That’s the beauty of it. At first, we thought it was sure to be a dealbreaker, but when we did the initial focus group trials only one in every hundred people even noticed. Of course, they’re working on upgrades as we speak so the zombie issue will soon be a thing of the past.”

“Too cool.” She watched as he tapped his wrist again, making his mega-me evaporate just as quickly as it had appeared.

“So, you didn’t say yet. Where are we headed? Or are you keeping up your big reveal till the very end?”

“Moriarty’s.”

“Moriarty’s?”

“Yeah, it’s this really great place on the corner of Fifteenth and Wellington. I gathered from when we spoke at my office that you might not go for the overseas trip thing yet, so I made a reservation at one of my favorite local spots. The food is great! You’re gonna love it. Trust me.”

Hmm… Not entirely sure she did trust him. Yet. She decided to reserve judgement until she’d had an opportunity to get to know him a little bit better.

“Oh, sorry.” His comms started beeping. “Do you mind? I really need to take this.”

“Oh yeah, sure. Go right ahead.”

She turned to enjoy the view of the city from her window.

Chapter 5

Leviticus 26:19
And I will break the pride of your power; and I will make
your heaven as iron, and your earth as brass...

"Okay. Go right ahead. Dig in!" He waved a hand across the table.

And now, just a few minutes after arriving at the restaurant, she knew exactly why those
"Trust me" words had struck such a note of dread in her mind.

"I'm dying to hear what you think." He gestured to the plate the waiter had just set in front of her, laden with cheesy looking potatoes, a selection of aromatic cuts of meat, and mouth-watering veggies.

That she hadn't ordered.

That *he'd* requested for both of them. Before they'd even got there. To save time. And apparently because he knew he'd be spending more of it speaking with someone in his administration than to her. Obviously, his interpretation of 'dying to hear' what she had to say was vastly different from hers.

"Something wrong with yours?" He said around

his third…or tenth, big forkful. "Mmm…sooo good." He shoveled in another.

"Uh…no. It's fine. Thank you." She picked up her knife and fork, cut off a small piece of potato and tried it. He was right. It was really very good.

"Doesn't sound fine. One minute I'm telling Vincent he can bring us dinner and the next you're like this?" He put down his fork as he looked across the table at her. "Oh crap, don't tell me. I'm like the biggest meat eater in the galaxy and you're what? Like a vegetarian, or something? Go figure." He gave a deep chuckle.

"Really? And so, what if I am? Why in the world would you think that was funny?"

"Oh, no, not you. I was laughing at myself 'cause it would be hilarious. You know? A meat eater and a vegetarian. I can hear it in my head. The start of at least a dozen of those 'walk-into-a-bar' jokes." He chuckled again.

She glared at him.

His eyes widened a bit and he cleared his throat.

"Uh…anyway. What is it then? Because I can order you something else, if you prefer."

"And there it is." She dropped her utensils, and they clattered against her plate. "Tell me, exactly when did you decide I lack the ability to select and then communicate my own choice of an entrée? Was it before, or after you bought the dress?"

"What?"

"You heard me. Because obviously if I'm fashion-challenged it stands to reason I probably couldn't be trusted to order a salad either, right?"

"I'm confused. So, you *are* a vegetarian?"

"No. I'm not, but that's not the point."

"Well, then please, enlighten me as to what is. Because I am straight-up clueless right about now."

"Look…we came here to discuss the plans for my nonprofit. So, let's just do that and get through this dinner. Shall we?"

"Get through…?"

He started to say something else, but the look she leveled on him next silenced him. He ate a few more bites and just as she recommended, turned his attention to the project for which she needed funding. And when he said he needed details, he wasn't joking.

He grilled and tested her. On every aspect. From the suitability and adaptability of the design plans for the new structures, to the staffing needs, and about short term as well as medium term concerns, she hadn't even considered, until he referenced them.

"Well, I have to say. I'm really impressed with what you've accomplished so far Elise. You are a true credit to that organization."

They made their way out of the restaurant and out onto the curb after dinner.

"Oh, it's a team effort. We have a great group of very competent people. I just coordinate. I'm sure they'd hardly even miss me if I weren't around. Everything would continue running just fine."

"Now, I know that's not true. You're being too modest, you know that, right? And that amazing vision for the future? I know you're not going to suggest that's not all your doing? Your brainchild? There's no doubt in my mind that if we back you, every dollar you get from my administration is going to be totally well spent, and all because of your intellectual property and its impact."

"Really? You're not just saying that?" She beamed.

"No. Trust me. I wish some of our upcoming projects were as well thought out and executed as what you've accomplished so far on just your starting shoe-string budget."

"Thank you, Senator. That means a lot to hear you say that."

"And I meant every word. Oh, and call me Finn, please." His smile was an invitation to so much more, when her head was already so giddy with his recent praise.

"Okay, well, let me just call the car around and I'll take you home."

Screeeeeeech!

Well, will you look at that. Looks like a whole passel of clueless sheep just ambled on over to join that really super unlucky cow.

"Excuse me?"

"The car. It's just in the parking garage of the restaurant. I'll call it over, so we can leave."

"Uh… No. Thank you. I can just catch a cab home. Goodnight." She raised her hand high and signaled to a hover-cab a short distance beyond the restaurant and started to turn.

"What? No. No. Not goodnight. Are you kidding me? Just like that?" He reached out and grasped her descending arm before she could make good her escape, as the self-driving vehicle pulled up in front of them.

He looked alarmed.

"Will you please…please, just talk to me? I feel like I'm about to have a serious case of whiplash with your mood swings tonight. This can't all be about the dress, or even me ordering dinner for us ahead of time. What is it? What's wrong? Tell me…please." He held onto her arm and turned her towards him.

"Nothing. It's fine. Thank you. For this evening. It was…an experience."

"Look, I don't really know you…yet, but that's definitely not nothing. Barring our first kiss, which was amazing by the way, and the first convo we had in the car, the rest of this entire night has been an air-rail wreck. Yes, oh yes, it has and you know it. Don't shake your head and try to deny it. And now…well, now your words just expressed gratitude, but your face is telling me a whole different story. So, come on, talk to me. If for no other reason than the fact we may well be working together closely for the next month, give or take, on this project. We need to at least be able to get along and be civil."

"Oh, so you were serious? You're really going ahead with the funding?"

"Of course, I am. I already told you; I fully endorse what you and your team are seeking to accomplish in our communities, and I meant it. Whatever else happens between us tonight doesn't change that."

Well, there you go. A man of rare integrity. She certainly hadn't expected that. Maybe she'd misjudged him?

She took in a deep breath. "Okay, see… It's just that it feels like you wanted me to look a certain way and be a certain way tonight. Like you prepared your little contingency plans just in case, to ensure it. First the dress, then the preset meal. And now…"

"What about now?"

"Now, you're trying to take me home even though I clearly said I didn't want you to meet me there tonight. This all just feels like I'm being handled, and I don't like being handled."

"Handled? What?" He released his loose hold on her arm. "Where is any of that even coming from? And I never said any of that. What you just said."

"Maybe not in those words, sure, but your actions tell a different story too. And what I heard, is what you're wearing isn't good enough, I don't credit you with enough intelligence to choose your own meal, *and* you didn't want me to come to your home, but joke's on you, 'cause guess what? I'm gonna invite myself over there anyway."

"Oh. Wow! Really?" He put a hand up to his forehead. "Are you kidding me with this right now? Look, you had me meet you at the shelter. I know how much work gets done there every day. Coordinating an operation of that size and complexity is no walk in the park and you are absolutely to be credited for all of that. I assumed you'd be super busy, so busy in fact, you might not have found the time to get home to change. So, sue me. I thought you might appreciate a nice dress. As far as the food goes, I wanted you to have a real sense of what I enjoy so much about one of my most favorite restaurants in the city, and call me crazy, I thought that would probably be best accomplished by having you eat the actual selection off the menu I enjoy so much. And since I picked you up from work,

I thought you might need a ride after. Go figure! This was not some dastardly plan to invade your home. That's not what this is. At all. You are being crazy! How could you even think that?"

Crazy! Oh, hell no! He did not just call me crazy!

"How could I…?! Let's review, shall we? First, you show up late, then you were on your coms half the night, at least when you weren't breadcrumbing me, the few times you actually deigned to speak to me."

"Breadcrumbing? What?! And I already told you I had–"

"Yeah, yeah. Important, high level, super-secret-security-spy-stuff. I heard you the first time. Oh, don't look at me like that. And please. Do not pretend like you don't know what I'm talking about. I read Trendsetter. You were late. On your coms all night. And breadcrumbing me?" She ticked off the list on three fingers. "That's like the 'how to spot a loser' trifecta right there."

"Loser? Really? Well, tell me, what did it say about women who are afraid of even a shadow of their own feminine power, huh?"

She gasped.

Then spun towards the hover-cab.

"Ah, darn it! I'm sorry. I shouldn't have said that. Wait. Elise?" He tried to grasp her arm, but she wrenched it away as she turned back to face him.

"Oh, no! We are done! It's Ms. Sharpe to you now. Because after that whole mess? Any chance you had of us being on a first name basis, ever again, evaporated with that last comment. In fact, if it weren't for my responsibility to get the funding for the nonprofit, I'd end our association entirely. Right here. Right now. But since that's not an option, I'd say we're firmly back in the 'strictly professional, address me by my title and last name' territory, wouldn't you?"

"No, I wouldn't, actually."

She glared at him then turned back to her ride.

"Wait. Just one minute, will you?"

She slid into her seat in the back of the cab.

"Thank you again, for dinner, Senator. I'll be in touch with your admin with regards to first steps for the project we discussed." She watched the door close behind her. "Lock it up. NOW. Gladstone Mews, in Greenwich Village, please." She spoke her destination into the console of her hover-cab as she ignored the faint muffled sound of his protestations right outside, and the sight of his open palms pressing against, and disrupting the light gleaming off the latticed laser beam-reinforced glass window. She took in a ragged breath, sat back so the passenger forcefield could hem her in, and didn't look back, as the car lifted off the ground and sped off.

"Okay, so that was a spectacularly unmitigated disaster." She fell across her bed and faceplanted her comforter as soon as she got home.

"Arrrggg!" she fake-screamed, and half growled into the soft bedding.

Flipping over, she laced her fingers across her midsection.

Would it be an exaggeration to say that was her worst night out in recent history? In fact, her worst ever. She thought back on the series of mishaps, misstatements, and near misery of the entire encounter from start to finish and knew it wasn't.

And to think, after their first meeting she'd been so worried he'd be so irresistible she'd have to reign in her passion, control her response to his charm and animal magnetism. Have to exercise herculean restraint to not…what had he said? Oh yeah, "initiate" anything.

What a joke!

More like she needed to restrain herself from calling an early halt to the disaster enfolding, and from bolting out of the restaurant as fast as her legs would carry her. Only her decent upbringing and respect for his good office prevented her from doing just that. Fortunately, he'd been true to his word, confirming that regardless of what happened between them, he fully intended to go ahead with the funding for her nonprofit.

How had it all gone so wrong so fast?

She thought they'd shared a moment in his office that first day, and real chemistry. More than she'd felt with anyone…since Danny.

How dare he say she was afraid of her own power?

She wanted to be furious with him for making that statement, but deep inside she knew the reason why it had hurt so much was because he was right. Inside she *was* afraid. Afraid enough, that obviously and to her eternal shame, he'd been able to discern it. Even in the very short time they'd been together.

Afraid…

In her job and in her personal life.

Of being seen to be taking just a bit too much

credit for the success of her business. Being so competent that her actions got mislabeled as arrogance by people who didn't know any better. Her passion, seen as the aggression of just another pushy, insufferable, head 'you-know-what' in charge.

Afraid…

To feel again. To stand in that humbling, extraordinary space where you just knew without a doubt you commanded the love, respect, and utter devotion of another human being.

Oh, yes. She was afraid all right. Afraid to be that woman again, with any man.

Because maybe…just maybe, she'd lose that man too.

Now here she was, questioning everything. About herself, about him. Well…not everything. Her mind went back to their amazing kiss before dinner. Real and explosive. There was absolutely no denying that. She shivered in the best way, as she relived the feel of his fingers caressing the nape of her neck, as he kissed every memory, of every single past kiss, into oblivion. And with that, came that hint of discomfort. A twinge of a feeling she was being disloyal to Danny. Because when he'd given her his kisses, even into their early twenties, they'd been like those of an eager and attentive teenager.

While Finn kissed like a man.

A man experienced, absorbed, and intent.

Intent on having her.

Like she was his best, most treasured fantasy. And one he was determined to turn into a reality.

How could someone who was just so completely awful and wrong for her, give kisses so yummy and right?

And consuming.

Wow...

It was baffling.

Clearly, she'd completely misread him. She'd thought his comment about how and where he'd take her out, compelling, racy, and hot. When instead, she should have been thinking, stalker-much? And sketch as all hell! Just like what she'd thought about his nano-guardian when he'd activated its display feature. She was probably actually very lucky he really wasn't a dang serial-killer.

"And what about Moriarty's? Wasn't that the name of Sherlock Holmes's infamous archrival," she wondered aloud. "Really? I shoulda known."

If that wasn't a red flag, she didn't know what was.

She sighed, shook her head, and dragged herself up to go get ready for bed.

"Wow. I've seen it on a gazillion, multiplied by a gazillion occasions, but Legion sure don't play when they set out to mess with one of the beloved, do they?"

"I know that's right. They sure did a number on Elise, *and* on Finn tonight. No doubt. It was tough to watch, but I knew I couldn't step in. She'll be all the better for it. They both will. Especially if he's not the one for her. His perfect will be done." Kai bowed his head and smiled as he took in a deep and reverent breath.

"All things work together. Amen." Archangel Raphael nodded. "And take heart brother because a Father, Creator, Spirit-sized, joy-filled, healing blessing is coming with her name on it. Like she'd never believe. I'll make sure of it." He slapped him on the back, right before he disappeared.

Kai took great comfort in those words. The thing about being an angel was that you never knew what you were being called to, well, until you knew. Each of them played their own role in the Creator's perfect will, plan, and timing. Working in perfect harmony and in well-orchestrated balance.

So, there was, for example, the miracle of Sandalphon, who carried music in his very body. A literal instrument of constant, glorious, and inspired praise. In heaven and on the earth. Then there was Uriel, blessed to inspire wisdom and philosophical illumination, and to quite literally reflect the matchless light of God. And Michael. Made to be the ultimate warrior and destroyer of evil, wielding the inexhaustible power of the Three in One, and just crushing Legion's forces of darkness, left and right, in all the many fallen dimensions of the world. While Raphael was their specially designed vehicle of healing and compassion. Bringing with him physical, emotional and spiritual wellbeing to all of mankind. Joy, even laughter, comfort and the all-encompassing peace that passes all understanding, to guard their hearts and minds in deep and abiding fellowship with the Creator.

Yes. Elise was in good hands. No doubt. Plus,

the God-inspired pairing hadn't escaped him. Elise, much like Raphael, was in her own small way well versed in providing caring, loving resuscitating service to a fallen planet earth, and all its hurting inhabitants. Bringing them together would be a critical catalyst in her life. The one that would spark an eternal and everlasting flame of faith.

Yes. They were about to make a very good team indeed, and he for one, couldn't wait to see it all unfold.

Chapter 6

1 Corinthians 13:13
And now abideth faith, hope, love, these three; but the greatest of these is love...

"Good morning, Ms. Sharpe? I'm calling from Senator Berring's office."

"Hi. Gretchen, right?"

"Yes. You remembered."

"Yes. Of course. How are you today?"

"I'm good. Thank you for asking. I hope you're well too. Listen, I'm just calling to confirm you received a package from the senator. He asked me to get it to you right away. You left it in his car after your meeting last night?"

"Oh, yes, I got it this morning." She reached out and fingered the box sitting on her desk. A gorgeous, yet still stark reminder of their disastrous dinner. "But there was no need for him to send it all the way over here. Really. Please tell him I plan on returning it."

"No. So that's not happening. I'm sorry, I mean,

he also said if you protested, even in the least, I should tell you that you absolutely must accept it as his most sincere apology. He said not to take no for an answer."

"Okay, well…fine then." She didn't want to argue with the admin. She was just doing her job, after all. "Please, be sure to tell him I said thank you."

"Great! Will do. Also, regarding the expansion of your nonprofit and how it will all unfold. The senator also asked me to reach out to you to send us your infrastructure plans, detailed budgets and scheduling of any preliminary meetings with the project manager, any independent contractors, and such. Pretty much everything pertaining to what's planned over the next two months, as a start. He's really busy, as you would imagine, so I'll try my best to carve out some time in his agenda to synch up with the timing of the occasions and for the activities he needs to be a part of initially. Then I'll step in to keep him informed, and he'll decide what else he needs to sit in on, case by case, after that. So, I'd really appreciate if you could please build in as much flexibility as possible as it relates to setting appointments well ahead of time?"

"Certainly, I fully understand what's involved, so I'll ensure we get at least two or three options for timing whenever we have to schedule a meet. And I'll get right on the other stuff you asked for as well. You'll have everything by close of business tomorrow, if that's okay?"

"Yes, that'll be great. Thank you."

"Okay, looking forward to working with you, Gretchen. Thank you again, so much."

"Same here and you're welcome. Have a great day!"

"You too. Take care. Bye-bye."

"Well, I have to hand it to you."

"Huh?" She looked over at Chaz who was looking comfortable, as he sat in her office as she took the call from the senator's admin.

Too comfortable.

Uh-oh…

"I mean, come on. Only you could so royally screw up a first date. Fall for the guy AND still manage to lock down a big payday for the shelter." He lifted the cover of the box on her desk and looked inside. Fingered the embossed card contained within. "Dior… Very nice indeed… For Elise: A unique creation, for a singular woman… So, let's review, shall we? A killer dress, *plus* a big payday? Cha-ching baby-girl! Now that takes real skill."

"You are so wrong right now, on so many levels. I can't even tell you." She slapped his hand away from the box then shook her head and frowned at his deep chuckle.

"What? We just discussed this. When you got home last night. Or did you forget? Did you, or did you not tank that date? Big-time. Huh?"

"First off, I told you it was not a date, and as far as tanking goes… Well, I'd say there was mutual uh…torpedoing that went down. On both sides."

"Not a date?! Are you kidding me with that right now? This is me you're talking to Lise. I know you. You in love with this dude, or what? You said it yourself. That what went down, was a kiss that rocked your no-nonsense-having, God-loving, non-profitmaking, and now…Dior designer dress-owning world. AND nearly off your brand-new stilettos."

"What? Where do you even get this stuff? I said no such thing." She straightened her jacket and shifted in her seat as she tried to recall their exact conversation the night before. "What I think I said was that it was a really great kiss, as…uh…kisses go."

"So, I paraphrased a bit. Same thing."

"No-ooo. Oh, no. Did you even hear what you just said? That was most definitely not the same thing."

"Whatever. I know you. Just look me in the eye. Right now. And tell me that boy Finn did not make you forget your dang name with that kiss, girl."

"What?!" She burst into laughter, grateful he'd closed the door to her office on his way in, so everyone on the main floor wouldn't hear her unprofessional behavior.

"See? I know you–"

"Yeah, yeah, so you know me. So what? I think we've covered that ground, don't you?"

"This is exactly what I mean. Just listen to you. You! Getting all defensive and with the girly-giggles at the very mention of his name, when you and I both know you are not the girly-giggle type. Come on now. A blind man could see it. Hell, Barry saw it. He told me when I left the office last night, and he *is* dang-near blind, as old as he is. Aww yeah… You are whipped, girl! It's clear as day."

"What's clear is, I obviously tell you *way* too much about my personal life."

"Ha! See? There you go again. You said

personal life. Thought it was *A business meeting,* and not a date, huh?"

"Okay, that's it…get out. I have work to do."

"All right, all right. I'm going." He stood up. "But just tell me…" His voice lowered to its sexy-gravel best. He leaned over her desk and put a hand to his chest to keep his tie in place.

"Uh-huh?" She turned away, to the right, as she pulled up her air screen. The electronic display rose up from the center of her desk, and she waved a hand to bring it closer.

"The fingers playing on the neck thing. Was it like, a brushing thing, or like a little tickle? Because yuh know I'm all about upping my game with Shelby."

"Are you kidding me right now?"

This was too much, even for him.

"No, no… I kid you not, Lise. So, could you just help a brother out and–"

"Consider yourself helped then. Out!" She laughed at her own joke as she gestured to the door.

"So, what are you saying? 'Cause I'm thinking your door's closed. Come on now…don't make me have to go look for the security curb-cam footage. How about a little demo? You could just–"

"Out I said! Go! Right now!" She yelled on a laugh.

Feeling her face heat at the memory of the senator's deft fingers playing her like a finely tuned instrument, and unable to meet Chaz's gaze, she kept her focus directly on the screen floating above her desk, and pointed towards her closed door.

"Yeah. You whipped." This time his receding

mumble and low chuckle, and the soft whistle of her door opening, confirmed his exit.

Chapter 7

James 5:16
Confess your faults one to another, and pray one for another, that ye may be healed. The effectual fervent prayer of a righteous man availeth much...

"Hey, Creamy-dreamy?"

"Huh?" Elise looked up from her e-inventory of goods for distribution to various locations, as Chaz came through her office door. Feeling like he'd never left, she shook her head as his words sunk in.

"You heard me. Haven't taken your nose out of that air screen in weeks. Skipping lunch in the breakroom. It's just like I said, you still whipped, Lise. What else am I supposed to call you? Aww yeah…that name is def gonna stick. Especially if you keep acting the part." He grinned on a chuckle as he tucked his long, lean, and gorgeous frame into one of the chairs in front her desk.

"Seriously?" She got ready to launch into one of their comfortable, familiar, albeit slightly annoying of late, tit-for-tat exchanges, but then abruptly changed her mind. "You know what Chaz? Whatever. Clearly, you're starved for entertainment, at my expense. So go on ahead, be my guest. Enjoy yourself. I'll just be over here getting some actual work done. How about that?" She glared at him then went back to sorting through her listing.

"Woah, okay, so that was different. Come on now, you know how we do. Why aren't you doing what we do baby-girl?"

Hearing the note of sincerity and love in his voice, she sighed and looked up from her screen.

"It's just still a little strained between us, me and the senator I mean, so I'm not really up to joking about it. Know what I mean?"

"Hey, I'm sorry Lise. I didn't think it was *that* bad between you two. Wanna talk about it?"

"We had that initial meeting, remember? And it was weird. I mean, I was uncomfortable, and I think he was too. It felt like we were both walking on eggshells, afraid to say the wrong thing. Thank God the project manager kept us both engaged in answering like a million questions. Well…mostly him."

"He's smart as a whip, isn't he? Come on, tell the truth."

"Even more than that. He is brilliant! Like a regular Albert Einstein. Darn it!"

"Uh-huh. Told yuh." Chaz chuckled.

"So, anyway, all the questions and the back and forth, that was the *only* reason I think either of us was able to get through it. And he looked so sad too, at times whenever I caught him looking at me, yuh know? Maybe about something else–"

"But you just know it was all about you. Right?"

"Exactly! I kept wondering if he felt the awkwardness between us and it upset him, and then all those thoughts I've been having about whether I misjudged him just kept resurfacing. And you should have seen him, that adorable look of his, with the messy-sexy hair–"

"And you just wanted to kiss him again, to see if you imagined it, or if he'd blow your mind again, like he did that night?"

"Yes! Only no. Because that would be wrong, right? I don't even think I like him, given what I know now."

"You mean what you think you know. Hey, I say go for it. That kind of instant chemistry between you two…it's rare. Believe me. Why don't you call him up? He gave you his digits, didn't he? See if he suggests a do-over…and for pity's sake, will you just give the guy a break this time? Maybe don't dissect every little word he says and go off on him like he's got some kind of ulterior motive, or hidden agenda. Has it occurred to you that since that night, maybe he has just as many misgivings about you? After your little dinner-date-meeting-but not really, fiasco?"

"Of course it has. You know me. I've done nothing but rehash it in my head like a gazillion times! Analyzing every word, every nuance and expression on his face for what he's really like. For any clue about what he thinks of me… And that kiss…woah. Yuh know… I think I remember him saying it was amazing and–"

"Yeah, and what about the kiss? The fact that you keep coming back to it, and it–"

"Might mean exactly nothing. Right?"

"Or maybe…it means exactly everything…"

That gave her pause.

"Either way, the *only* way you're gonna know is if you talk to the guy and give him another chance."

"I guess. You're probably right."

"You know I am."

"Except…maybe I should wait a while. Right? Yuh know, just until we get the project up and running. If he really is as wrong for me as I think, I wouldn't want to antagonize him, and jeopardize the funding and all. The last meeting was an air-rail wreck too. At the end of it he kind of intimated that since he'd seen what he needed to go forward, we're at the stage where he can delegate the in-person stuff to his admin. Well, that and because some new national security matter is going to be demanding a lot more of his time. Don't even know if that's true."

"Oh, it is. I read something about that online."

"Well, true or not, clearly, he can't even stand being in the same room with me for an hour. Far less for all the different meetings that will be necessary over the next six months? Anyway, what do I care? It's like I said, I really don't think he's right for me. Not like Danny was. He and I…well, we couldn't be more different and–"

"And *you*…Elise Sharpe, are a straight-up scaredy-cat, yuh know that?" He shook his head as he frowned at her.

"I know, right?" She barked out a wry laugh, as he joined in with a dry chuckle.

"But for real though. There's no rush with love Lise." His expression and deep brown gaze turned serious. "If this is meant to be, or not, you'll know it, when you're ready. Chances are you'll just find yourselves right back together, where you need to be. These things just have a way of working themselves out. If you're faithful. So sure, give it a minute. Let the Spirit guide you. You'll know it. If, or when, the time is right."

"Wow, when'd you get all super spiritual."

"Excuse you? Have you even met my wife? The head of the church choir, the mother's union, the Wednesday evening prayer group, and every charity potluck held in the last ten years?"

"Point taken."

"Uh-huh. Trust and believe. It was bound to rub off. Me and mine, we are good in the Lord." He reached over her desk for a fist bump.

She grinned and met him halfway. "Seriously though. It always felt like Danny was the one dragging us both to faith, whether we liked it or not."

"Yeah, well…you've got me now. I'm here. For real Lise. I didn't want to press you too much. Especially with Danny gone and all. But now that you're back in church and renewing your walk, if you need a little support, just call. I'm serious. Any place. Any time. Plus, you know Shelby, she'll step in and be your prayer warrior every time."

"I know that's right."

She took in a deep breath and blew it out.

"Maybe I should just set my sights lower."

"Huh?"

"You know, to a really normal guy. Not some lady-killing, egotistical, high-ranking, even higher-rolling, GQ-holo type. Just a nice, sweet, decent…

Well…at least average looking though… 'cause–"

"You know yuh really don't wanna have to put a bag over his head?"

"For real. 'Cause…let's not get crazy. Am I right?"

"I heard that."

"So, an okay looking, hardworking guy who'll treat me good. Who I can come home to after a hard day at work. Can't you just see it…? I'll make dinner–"

"Although it'll be a bonus if he's the one who cooks."

"I know, right? Then we'll sit and enjoy a little screen time–"

"While he massages your tired, crusty, old feet."

"Really?" She barked out a laugh and pretended to throw her notetaker at him. "Can't hurt though, right?" She giggled.

"Hey, I'm all about that with Shelby. Don't tell her I said that, by the way."

"No, of course not. So, we enjoy a nice classic TV show, or movie…before we get ready for bed and–"

"And then *you* get ready for him to throw you up against your antique wooden bedroom door, as he rocks your secret-freak-loving world."

She gasped.

He clapped his hands together and roared with laughter.

"Dang, dude, I told you about that in confidence. Seriously?"

"Just like in your fave romance novel. Or wait…is it in your imagination? The ones you read don't actually go that far, do they?"

"Okay. That's it. That is the last time I tell you anything so–"

"Oh, girl please. Stop lyin'. You know you'll be telling me that and more once you get this Mr. Average on the hook. Who the hell else you gonna talk to. You know good and heaven well I'm your best friend in the whole dang world."

"Yeah, you are. I love you!" She jumped up and ran around her desk and immediately got pulled into one of those warm bear hugs of his.

"Love the way you slipped right into the good girlfriend finishing my sentences thing, by the way," she said as she pulled away and retook her seat. "You get an A-plus for that performance."

"Hey, most improved drama student. Right here," he jabbed a thumb towards his chest.

"Two years running." They both said and grinned.

"You were good too. How did you ever end up in content creation? I thought for sure you would have been getting accolades for your acting on some award show somewhere."

"Yeah, well, what can I say, life happens," he shrugged.

"Just as well. I can barely stand you now. You would have been ridiculous if you'd made it in front of the camera, instead of behind it."

"You mean you just wish you had all this." He flexed his biceps. "Too bad, you're not my type."

"HA! HA! Funny man," she fake-laughed. "Now get out. You and your impressive muscles, before I call security. I've–"

"Yeah, yeah. You've got work to do. I know the drill."

He headed to the door with a deep chuckle then turned back, his face serious.

"Remember what I said? Any place. Any time, yeah?"

"Yeah."

She smiled and blew him a kiss.

He pretended to catch it one-handed, and returned her smile, as he put the same hand over his heart.

Chapter 8

Psalms 23:4
*Yea, though I walk through the valley of the shadow of
death, I will fear no evil: for thou art with me; thy rod
and thy staff they comfort me…*

Archangel Raphael." Kai put his right fist over his heart for a moment, then urged her forward.

Woah…

She'd thought that Kai was striking in a T-shirt and jeans. But Raphael…well…he made him look like any old everyday Joe, by comparison. Because before her now, stood a gorgeous, black Adonis personified.

In board shorts.

Reminiscent of that 21st century actor Aaron Pierre. Only, with long, curly locks, and way bigger. Built like a South Korean, Black Panther battle tank. Only, way more beautiful.

She melted within the bright warmth of his perfect smile.

Got lost, wanting to completely immerse herself in the depths of the endless blue of his shining, crystal eyes, and not care if she *ever* got out.

Remembering her manners, she gathered her scattered wits and extended her hand.

"What? None of that. Come on now, bring it in here Lise!" He pulled her to him.

"Oh!" She all but tumbled into his embrace and it was amazing! A magnificent bear hug, to end all bear hugs. She was spoilt for all others from now on. Sorry Chaz. Even more powerful a sensation than when she shook Kai's hand on that fateful day, hugging Raphael felt like someone had just dunked her in a big ol' tub of 'feel-nothing-but-fabulous!'

Peace and unadulterated joy. On steroids. Washed over and through her.

Like her first birthday party as a child, opening the doors of the non-profit's first shelter.

And chocolate.

Lots and lots, like a never-ending supply of really, *really,* good quality chocolate.

"And uh…who's this?" When he released her, she took a few steps back and turned towards the guy she just noticed was standing quietly next to him. Curious, she took her time taking in his appearance, from head to toe. Well, that and the fact she needed to distract herself from a near overwhelming compulsion to jump right back into the best arms she'd ever inhabited. Again, and yet again.

Well, this was definitely no angel. He was average height. Not much taller than she was, actually. Looked middle-aged and was balding. What little hair he had, past his receding hairline, was brown and cut low. She wouldn't exactly call him appealing, but his appearance wasn't all bad. Overall, he was neat and clean, though he still managed to look kinda frumpy. And odd.

Two words popped into her mind – Awkward. And shady.

"Hi, I'm Archibald. You can just call me Archie." He gave her a hesitant smile and extended a hand that appeared to be glistening…with moisture?

"Okay, Archie. Right. Hi! And you can call me Lise." She smiled and gave him a little wave instead of a handshake. "I'd like to say it's nice to meet you, but under these circumstances, it's actually more like really weird to meet you like this."

"Yeah, I get that." He pulled his hand back and gave her an even more timid smile in return. "So, Raphael, you said you'd explain why we're here, when we were all together?" He turned to the angel.

"Yes. The exiles are getting close to a pivotal milestone in their plan. We'd like you both to work together to slow them down."

"I'm sorry, who?" Elise interjected.

"Oh, right. It's just what our brotherhood of angels calls them. You know them as the alien lifeform Verndari. In reality, they are the one-third who left our ranks eons ago and were cast down to earth."

"Exiles. I get it. Clever." Archie seemed impressed, while the alarm bells in her head went from the little clock on her bedside table to Big

Ben.

The defenders were fallen angels?! How was that possible, and why was she only hearing about this now? She wondered how many other people knew and decided to put every single one of her questions to Kai when next they were alone. Meanwhile…

"Say no more. I'm in. How can we help?" Archie sounded his agreement right away as he leaned to his left and picked up a glass off a nearby table that suddenly appeared in her line of vision. He put it to his waxy looking lips and took a big, noisy gulp.

"Hold on. Take it easy there, eager beaver. I'd like to hear a little more before *WE* agree to help with anything." She turned to Raphael, "You and Kai are both pretty powerful angels, so what do you need us for? No offence."

"None taken, and the simple answer is, this is for your benefit, not ours."

"This entire fight is not ours. The battle is already won in heavenly places, Lise. Remember?" Kai's gentle touch on her arm drew her gaze to his bright blue one.

"Okay, and I understand that, so what are you saying? That we have to face down these…exiles, on our own?" She turned back to Raphael.

"No, naturally we'll be here to help and guide you, every step of the way."

"But what are we supposed to do, if they roll up on us? Like in here. Now."

"Fear not. Darkness cannot exist within light. And we carry the light of the Three in One in abundance. They can't be in mine, or Kai's, or any angel's presence for that matter, unless the Creator expressly wills it."

"Here?"

"Anywhere. In every corner of the Creator's grand universe. Any dimension. Any time."

"Wow. Any dimension? How many are there?"

"You can't count that high." Kai reached over and tweaked her on the nose. He chuckled as she swatted his hand away.

"Ha. Ha." She fake-grinned at him, then giggled.

"What Kai means is, it's beyond the human brain's ability to comprehend." Raphael's voice was gentle, ringing with wisdom, empathy and calming reassurance.

"Okay, so you say they can't inhabit your light, but what if you're not around? What if we're all alone?"

"You are never alone Lise. Praying distance…is no distance at all… Remember…"

If ever a statement of deep-seated truth uttered by someone, could transcend space and time. Just take life and materialize, right before her eyes, into vivid, vibrant and memorable sight, and sound. Then this was that truth. And Raphael, the someone.

Hands down, the single most powerful phrase she'd ever heard. Delivered by one whose unquestionable connection and complete allegiance to Almighty God called out to her to join in joyous surrender. Without reservation.

Drawn into the crystal-clear blue depths of his gaze. Like a moth to flame. Like a visual representation of the hallelujah chorus, it all resonated with her at a level and to a degree she'd never, ever forget. With or without his closing exhortation to her recall facility.

"So, I'm confused." Archie broke into her reverie as he rejoined their discussion. "If they can't be where you are, and I'm assuming that's also the case when they're posing as Verndari on earth. Then why all this?" He waved the hand that wasn't holding the tiny umbrella-decorated, fruity tropical drink, to indicate the gorgeous white-sand beach in Negril, Jamaica, where they were standing. "Why not just appear to us in the regular earthly realm?"

"Well, we could, but it would have probably freaked you out. Big time."

"Okay, so that's a fair point."

"Yeah, not sure that would have been my idea of a good time either. For real." Elise nodded as she considered what such an encounter might have been like. It was difficult to explain, but even on the occasions before she knew who he was, when she'd met Kai in the dream realm, even though some of the odd circumstances had seemed very real, she hadn't been scared.

As gorgeous as he might be, she honestly didn't know if that would have been the case if he'd just popped up in her office, or God forbid, her house, on some random Tuesday.

"And just look at where we are." Raphael spread his arms wide as he beamed. "You can't tell me enjoying this kind of mini vacation isn't a bonus, huh? I'd say this D.I.E.T. beats taking a meeting sitting in some stuffy old office somewhere, anytime. Am I right?"

"All day long!" Kai's response was effusive as he bumped light-filled fists with him.

She took a moment to enjoy the unusual way they demonstrated their unique connection with God, and the sheer power of His light, then she looked around.

Well, she couldn't argue with that logic.

Up above, the sky was as blue as she'd ever seen it. A gentle breeze every now and again was doing its job to take the edge off the tropical heat. Straight ahead, the near musical, soft lapping of gentle swells rolling into shore, on white coral sand, was met with the cheerful shrieks of both children and adults. Off to the right, some people were getting suited up for various watersports, and for an exhilarating looking swing on the nearby trapeze apparatus. There they all were, enjoying the beautiful, calm azure water, and the gorgeous bright sunny day.

"Not to mention, this is the best way of getting you two together–"

"Huh?" She wondered if she'd misheard Raphael's last words, given how distracted she'd been, but then eyed Archie as he simultaneously made a slight choking sound.

"Excuse me?" His voice squeaked.

"Together, at the same time, confidentially discussing what needs to be done to thwart the Vernadari agenda. For sure, the exiles can't be around us while we're sitting in a digital horse-drawn buggy in Central Park, or in a trendy restaurant, but unfortunately, misguided, traitorous people can." Raphael explained.

"Oh, right." She signaled her understanding.

"Yeah, that makes logical, practical sense," Archie nodded.

He dabbed at the beads of sweat that popped out on his reddened forehead, and she wasn't sure if she should be relieved at the Archangel's clarification, or offended that Archie seemed to be more discomfited by the idea of them being together, than she was.

Of course, it could just be that he was shy and wouldn't be brave enough to approach her like that. Hmm… There was no ring on his left hand. But did jewelry even make it into this dream realm? She touched her neck and automatically followed the links of her chain right to Danny's ring dangling at her chest. Okay, so chances are if he had a ring, she'd have seen it. Plus, he didn't look married, did he? Well… It was obvious he wasn't exactly Mr. Swinging-single. Maybe she'd simply misread his reserved manner, for awkwardness?

"So…" she dragged her gaze away from Archie and addressed Raphael. "You said something about a milestone in their plan? What plan? And what do you need us to do exactly?"

"They're in deep with certain high-ranking members of the current administration, and they've been secretly lobbying to get the age of chip implantation down."

"Down to what?" Archie's question was sharp.

"Twelve."

At Raphael's response, he paled. Looked like he was about to be sick.

She put a hand up to her mouth, feeling her own stomach churn at the thought.

"But it's eighteen now. Adults. Who are equipped to make that kind of life-changing decision. A twelve-year-old child can't handle that branding thing they do. What parent would agree to that? No. No way. They can't do that."

"I'm afraid they can, Lise. And a child of that age will be able to walk right into one of their centers and elect to get it. With, or without their parents' consent." The angel's expression turned grim.

"So, what are we talking about? Is this planned age change just here, in New York?" Archie wondered.

"No. Country, then world-wide, if they have their way."

"But you can't even walk into a store and buy a pack of cigarettes until you're twenty-one in this country. Are you telling me they're gonna make it so that a child, barely into their teens, can go get burned and disfigured?" Elise was horrified.

Then it hit her.

"So, the rumors are true? It's the mark…of the beast, isn't it?" She whispered the words, afraid to say them out loud.

Raphael nodded, a deep sadness settling onto his features.

"But they don't know what they're doing, the people who are accepting it."

"They do. Verndari make sure of it." The angel's expression went from sad to grim.

"But they can't know what it means."

"I'm sorry, but they do Lise. Unfortunately, some are ensnared by the temporary trappings of this world. They'll do anything to get them." She spun towards Kai at his softly spoken words.

"No. It's self-preservation. They're starving. They're only taking it because they have no choice."

"You wouldn't."

"What?"

"Even if you didn't know...you'd never take it. You said so yourself. You'd rather starve because deep down inside you know it's wrong, if it will cost you your eternal soul."

She inhaled deeply. Compressed her lips to make them quit their trembling. Blinked and willed away the tears that threatened to spill over and fall.

Raphael's breath came out on a heavy sigh. "It'll require a two-thirds majority vote in Congress to get passed into law. And it's happening soon, unless we do something."

"So, we make sure it doesn't get that support, right?" She looked around at the solemn faces surrounding her. "I know someone in the administration who I think can be trusted to help." She rubbed a hand across her teary eyes, and forehead under her bangs. "It's just we aren't exactly on good terms right now."

"Well, leave that part to me then, I've got connections in government who I think will be willing to give me a hearing on how serious this is, and how important it is to stop it," Archie chimed in.

"Lise?" Raphael touched her arm. "Can you use

your charitable apparatus to ramp up donations for the families who rely on your shelters and food supply?"

"Yes. Of course. And I heard what you said, but I still think the more people that don't get tempted to make the wrong choice the better, so I'll make that a top priority."

"What about your friends in conscious media? In the Underground? Can you get any of them to help get the word out about the plans to change the implantation age? The exiles thrive in lies and shadows, the more you can bring this to light the better."

"Absolutely! Yes, I can do that too. As it happens, I have a friend who's in mainstream media, but also in the Underground, she goes by the handle Cynical in NYC. She's been trying to out the defenders for the fake saviors they are for nearly a decade now. This is right up her alley. I'm sure she'll help us. People need to be told about what's going on. No right-thinking American is gonna just roll over and let this happen. We can start a groundswell of opposition. There's no way they can go forward with this if people let their representatives at state level know they won't stand for it."

"Good." Raphael nodded. "I'm truly sorry this first meeting was such a downer, you two. But it had to be done. No way around it."

"Just ripped that plaster right off, didn't yuh?" Lise sniffed and dabbed at the residual wetness on her lashes with the back of her hand.

"Plaster? That was more like getting a root

canal with a rusty drill, AND no Novocaine." Archie's tone was dry.

"Yeah. Good one Archie," she giggled, feeling better.

"Okay, so now we've got the unpleasantries out of the way, I feel like I owe you guys a do-over for ruining our lovely day at the beach. Who's up for a brand new D.I.E.T.?" Raphael grinned.

Lise raised her hand high into the air, just in case Archie had the same thought. She'd be hogtied to a stubborn mule before she let him beat her out in the fantasy dream queue.

"And we have a winner! Yes, Lise. Let me guess…afternoon tea at a certain outdoor café in Nice?" Raphael pointed in her direction.

"Aww yeah. Make mine a double portion of those great pastries, please. Kai knows the drill. Oh, and some ice cream."

"Ice cream? Pastries? Did you say Nice? As in the south of France? Is that wise?" Archie looked more and more hesitant as he issued his barrage of questions. "I was thinking maybe we could just head back. It's been a long night…I think… I dunno, guys. Hasn't it?"

"Aww…is this your first time travelling?" She could tell from the look on his face it was. "That's so sweet."

"Uh…no. I've actually been overseas before."

"No, silly," she giggled. "I mean this kind of nighttime, in your dreams *travelling*. You know? The way the angels do it."

"The way the angels do? What? I just figured I'd wake up and–"

"Oh-ho-ho! No, my friend, you are in for a really special treat tonight. Trust me, you're gonna love this." She grasped his arm and gave it a reassuring pat. "Here, hold onto my arm though 'cause yuh might wanna brace yourself this first time. Angel dream-hopping can be kinda dicey."

She looked to Raphael and Kai and they all shared a grin.

"What?! What's that look mean? Anyone? Guys? Wait–"

SNAP!

She was pretty sure his ear-splitting scream echoed across all those dimensions Raphael *hadn't* told them about.

Chapter 9

James 1:17
Every good gift and every perfect gift is from above, and cometh down from the Father of lights, with whom is no variableness, neither shadow of turning...

"Yuh know, anybody ever tell you, yuh scream like a little girl."

"Yeah, my wife. Every time she does this amazing little trick she does with her–"

"La-la-la-la-la." She sang and stuck her fingers in her ears. "I'm *still* not interested in any of your sleazy stories, Chaz."

"Sleazy? Bite your tongue baby-girl. I'll have you know, my loving is never sleazy."

They shared a grin.

"Okay, so what gives?"

He moved away from her open doorway and dropped into one of the chairs in front of her desk.

"And do I need to remind you again that this is a place of business? When I heard you scream just now, I thought you were getting attacked, or something. What? Did Sheila finally catch up with you for jacking her soda pop out of the fridge last week?"

He opened his mouth and she held up a hand "Boy please, don't even try it. You know you're guilty as an 18th century wild, wild west bandit facing a firing squad at high noon."

He made a face.

"What? Too much?"

"And so riddled with historical inaccuracies, I can't even begin to tell you. How about you leave the drama AND the comic relief to me?"

"Really? Okay, noted. I will do that," she did a quick salute with her hand at her temple.

"Dang, I forgot how bad you used to do in history class. That right there was a flashback I did not need. Like, remember that project we had on the French Revolution of 1789 and you thought it was the French Fashion Revolution of 2055? Now that was embarrassing…and hilarious. You remember that?"

"So, anyway… What's up with the screaming in the middle of the busy workplace?" She gave him 'the look'. The one that meant he needed to get back on topic, pronto.

"Oh, right. Please, tell me I do not need to do content for all this." He flung a digital credit across her desk.

"Wait…does that say what I think it does?" She stopped its rapid slide, then used her thumb and forefinger to magnify it on the desk, unable to believe her eyes.

"Yep. Sure does."

"Fifteen million dollars?!"

"Oh yeah! Good old American moolah. We're talking bank! Cha…and ching, baby-girl!"

She screamed, jumped up from behind the desk and flung herself into his arms as he stood up. He held her, or at least tried to, as she bounced up and down within his loose embrace.

"Who's it from?" She looked at it again as she quieted and retook her seat.

"No clue. Jeremy, in accounting, he just brought it over. He said it came from an anonymous donor."

"Do you know what this means?"

"I hope I know what it *doesn't* mean. That this is just the first of dozens of uber-rich people responding to our planned campaign to offer bonus content for larger pledges. 'Cause if it is, I'm gonna have to hire more staff."

"Well, we'll cross that bridge if and when we get to it. Right now, I'm just so grateful for this blessing."

"Uh-huh. Between this and the ten mil we got from your very generous boyfriend just last week–"

"Not my boyfriend," she sang.

"Semantics," he brushed off her denial.

"Like I told you already, I happened to mention to the senator that we really need to ramp up donations this month, and he offered to help. That's all."

"Lise, an offer to help is ten thousand bucks, not ten million. You could as well start deciding where to set up your wedding gift registry, and who's doing your rehearsal dinner laser light show."

"Is that really a thing now? I thought it was just

a passing fad.”

"Oh, trust me. It's most definitely a thing.”

"Interesting… Well, I won't be getting you to do it, that's for sure.”

"Please! You should be so lucky to get me. You know good and well you can't afford to pay my freelance light-programmer fee. I bill by the hour you know.”

"As if?!" She glared at him, then snorted on a laugh. "I'm just messing with you. Dude, you are so in.”

"You know it." They bumped fists across the desk. "Anyway, the way I figure it, with all of this, we're gonna be able to help another…what? Maybe three hundred or more households avoid that Godforsaken devil tattoo. For a while at least.”

Her desk coms beeped.

"Elise? Is Chaz with you?”

"Of course, Mel, where else would he be?”

He fake-grinned and made a face like when they were kids, that she promptly returned.

"Please tell him he's got an urgent call from Mr. Dorchester.”

"Okay, thanks Mel. Be right there. I'll take it in my office." He got up and pushed back the chair as she ended the call. "Remind me, we need to talk about promoting that girl.”

"Who? Melanie?”

"Yes. We have got to keep her happy, right here with us. Can't afford to lose her to any of the new age media houses. They'll snap her up if they find out just how good she is, and if we give them that chance. I'm telling you; she is a whiz at creating content to suit specific demographics and personalities. She's got this really super creative and intuitive mind. I don't know how she does it. It's like she can just look at someone and know exactly what they need. Freaks me out sometimes."

"Or maybe she's just a decent, kind, and considerate human being who *listens*, is thoughtful, responsive, and sensitive to her customers' needs?"

"Yeah…whatever. I don't even know what that means."

She frowned at him and shook her head as he grinned.

"So anyway, Trent liked the content she did so much, he wants to talk about a monthly commitment. And he wants to work with her exclusively. Next time you talk to your boyfriend–"

"Again. Not my boyfriend."

He eyed her and continued as though she hadn't spoken, "Just remember to thank him again for sending his rich friend our way. He's an honest to goodness decent guy too. And talk about a class act. When people talk about old money, well, let's just say Trenton Dorchester, III, the man is swimmin' in that aged cheddar. For real!"

She gave him an enthusiastic thumbs up, before he took a few long strides to the door.

"It's happening, Lise. The new accounts we're getting. That money right there," he pointed to the credit he'd left on her desk, "it's a Godsend, for real. Things are finally taking off the way we dreamed. Mark my words." He left her office.

Hmm…

Talk about a Godsend… Because other than the

senator, she'd only told a couple people so far about the new donation drive – Mrs. McKinsey, Jonathan Decamp, and–

She froze.

Archie…

Of course. She meets this mysterious, mild-mannered guy who's sympathetic, and aligned to the same cause as her. They're literally brought together by heavenly intervention. And within a month, the non-profit gets inundated with anonymous cash, from an equally mysterious donor?

Coincidence?

Not likely!

He obviously didn't have that kind of wealth himself, but big kudos to him for convincing someone else who did to donate. Whoever Archie was, he must have some serious juice to pull that off. He'd said he had connections in government. She didn't know his last name, so she couldn't google him. Not that she was any good at that internet-snooping-trolling thing, or whatever they called it nowadays. Chaz was the Google-guru, not her.

She wasn't sure she was willing to share her own full name either. They were getting to know each other pretty well during Raphael and Kai's dream treks. But she wasn't ready for that big a step. What if he googled her? There was no telling what he'd find. There were any number of links to her affiliation with her non-profit, and other similar organizations that made her and her life look as exciting as watching paint dry. To say nothing of the many less than flattering photos she'd taken over the years. She had no clue if she even looked like herself whenever they met in their little dream world. But from the half a dozen times she'd caught him watching her, when he thought she hadn't noticed, she could tell from the way he looked at her, he liked what he saw.

So, no. An exchange of names at that point was definitely not happening.

Only drawback though, was that it meant she'd still not get to know much about who he was. She didn't know where he worked, or what he liked to do when they were back in the real world.

Maybe it would be fun trying to figure it out?

"Yeah… Who exactly are you, Archie, and where is this going?" she whispered, and smiled, as she twirled and played with the electronic credit beneath her fingers.

Chapter 10

Philippians 4:7
And the peace of God, which passeth all understanding,
shall keep your hearts and minds through Christ Jesus...

Seated in Moriarty's around seven, Finn checked his messages and played with the social media feed under his fingers on the table as he waited for Vincent to bring him his dinner.

"Ah, there you are Vinny."

The plate his waiter set in front of him, as he finally arrived at his table, was laden with all his meaty favorites. The delicious aroma of grilled steak, lamb, and chicken, along with double-cheesy garlic potatoes wafted off the plate, making his mouth water.

"Oh man, tell the chef he's really outdone himself this time." He looked up. "This is so great. Looks and smells even more amazing than usual, thank you."

Ready to dig in, he looked down at the table again. But this time, instead of just the one plate, there were over a dozen more, covering every square inch of the space in front of him.

He looked up and the query he was set to issue died on his lips at the look of derision on the waiter's face.

"What? Don't tell me… Suddenly *you* think something's too much? But this is only a miniscule fraction of what you gave away. Isn't that right, Senator?"

"What?"

"Sure. Ten million. Wasn't it? The man with the big bucks! Thought you'd impress her, didn't you? Show her how generous you can be? Big man in the Upper House, just showering her with dough? So why not let *us* show you how it's done, right now. Because you know us. We always *aim* to please–"

Suddenly, out of nowhere he was hit, repeatedly and hard. He raised his hands trying to protect himself and also fend off whatever missiles were pummeling him in the head and torso, from all sides.

"…aim to please ourselves that is!" He heard Vincent's words then his low rumble of laughter.

Just as abruptly as it started the assault stopped, and hesitant, he lowered his hands and looked down.

What the hell? Were those dinner rolls?

Bread was everywhere. Littering the table and the floor all around him. He reached out and touched the hard crusty exterior of one of the rounded hunks of baked dough that had just hit him, unable to believe his eyes. He looked up again.

"But then, you know all about that, don't you? Pleasing yourself? Everything you do is all about you, right?"

"What is this?" He eyed Vincent. Saw nothing but callous disregard. "What's going on?" He looked around. The people who were seated near him at the tables in the restaurant had all turned towards him. Looking like zombies in some B-rated 20th century horror movie, they said not a word but stared, with expressionless, dull faces. He looked up again at the waiter who was still standing beside his table. Grinning at him now, like a maniac.

"What? Bread wasn't to your liking tonight, Senator?"

"Huh?"

"Why don't you try the soup instead, then."

He leered. His face distorting and twisting into some kind of bizarre looking caricature of the man he'd gotten to know pretty well over the last three years, and considered a friend.

"Bon Appetit!"

Whatever it was, grabbed the back of his head and pushed it down into a bowl that appeared right in front of him on the table. He struggled, tried to move his arms and couldn't, finding them effectively restrained behind his back by something. He squeezed his eyes shut, held his breath each time as his face was forcefully pushed into the thick warm liquid again and again. Feeling like his head would snap off his neck, he was pulled back up again, and he could do nothing but gasp for breath as he stared up into his torturer's evil countenance as he continued to sneer into his face.

"What? You didn't like the soup either? No? But we've seen you eat it more than a dozen times at least. It's your favorite, isn't it?"

"Dear God." He closed his eyes, acknowledging what he'd feared, that this was not his accustomed reality. This was the twisted version of it he'd been encountering recently at night, and could not recognize as such, until it was far too late.

"God? Oh, so now you think just because you're reading a bit of scripture these days that qualifies you to call on *Him*? Well get this through your thick skull," he sneered. "You're nothing. Less than nothing. Unworthy and worthless. *You*…will never do anything EVER to earn His favor," he snarled. "So, you may as well just give up now."

A flash of something he'd read just the night before popped into his head, and with it came a Holy Spirit inspired peace. He relaxed, opened his eyes, and looked up. Right into the face of evil, with a calm he knew wasn't his. "You're absolutely right," he shrugged

"What?" Like a bad computer program, the creature's features flickered, settled, then flickered again.

"I can't ever *earn* His favor, but I can place my complete trust in the only one…who has."

As Finn watched, its eyes darted around. Its face twisting, and reforming, and distorting again, even worse than before. More than a dozen times, and in as many seconds.

"We grow weary of this. Time for dessert," he heard multiple voices in his head this time and in rushed words. Recognizing the pretense was at an end. He steeled himself. Anticipating what came next, he took in a deep breath an instant before he felt not just his head this time, but his entire body, get

submerged in an ice-cold sticky mush. Some kind of pudding, or maybe ice cream he presumed. Struggling to free himself, he pushed up and managed to get his head above the level of the thick and sticky mess. He turned left then right. All around he was surrounded by…a gigantic bowl?

What now?

It sucked at his legs, like quicksand, pulled him under. Over and over, he fought his way back to the surface, as he gasped for breath. Only to be yanked under again. Beginning to tire, he sensed a new threat, as in addition to being pulled up and down like a yo-yo, he was now beginning to spin in a wider and wider circle. Like being in a swift moving whirlpool of icy cream…

And strawberries?

You have got to be kidding me.

He jerked to the left as two or three gigantic pieces of his favorite bright red fruit hit him in quick succession, almost knocking him back and under. Righting himself, he continued twisting and turning, feeling like he was spinning out of control around and around…until suddenly–

"Okay, I think it's gonna go with this last turn! It's almost there!"

Wait…was that really Elise's voice he heard in his head, or just some new form of evil torture?

"What'd you say?"

"Get ready for it!"

"What? Get ready for what?! Are you gonna pull me up?!" He tried to fight his way to the surface.

"I can't this time. I tried, but for some reason I can't fly over you."

"So, what are you gonna do?" He wondered if it would be like the flash of light that had taken him home the last time she saved him.

"This!"

"Arrgggg!" He heard his own shout in his mind and winced, as he hit his side. Flung sharply to the left at first, he then surged forward, as the entire bowl tipped over, and him with it.

"Umph!" He dropped down, then slid out. Right off the edge and out onto a hard surface. Arms and legs spread out and feeling like jelly, he pressed up on trembling forearms. At least far enough so he could flip himself over.

"Thank you, Lord." He made the sign of the cross with a shaky hand, then passed it over his face as he watched the offending bowl roll away from him, leaving a sticky trail on the floor as it went.

Gasping for every breath he took, he looked up into a fuzzy yet familiar pretty face, and his favorite smiling light blue eyes leaning over him.

"Well, just look who we have here. You okay there, Senator?"

"Really...?" He took in another deep breath even though he didn't actually need it to communicate with her in the way they did in the void. *"Tell me... Do I look okay to you, Ms. Sharpe?"*

"No, not especially. But then who's to say? I hear tell it's some people's fantasy to get buried in...uh...ice cream? Just like this." Something that sounded suspiciously like a little giggle erupted from her, straight into his mind. She compressed her lips and cleared her throat. *"Your favorite's strawberry,*

I take it?" She touched his cheek with an index finger. Put it up to her beautiful, soft, smiling lips, and then into her mouth. *"Hmm,"* she nodded in confirmation. *"Not bad...better than food usually tastes in here. Of course, I'm kinda partial to chocolate myself."*

"Seriously? We're really doing this right now?"

"What...? I know you prob'ly had a bit of a rough night so far but, hey! Look on the bright side. Your hair looks way better than usual. Especially nice tonight. Spiky with ice cream is actually a pretty good look for you. That's at least good to know, right?"

He felt the soft touch of her fingers as she brushed a clump of his hair to the right side of his forehead.

He stared up at her.

She adjusted his hair again. To the left this time. Tilted her head to the side. *"Very becoming. Looks really...uh...yummy."* She licked her lips then covered them with the beautifully manicured fingers of one hand as she stifled another giggle.

"Don't you dare... If you laugh at me right now, so help me... No..." He pointed a stern finger at her. *"Don't you do it. I'm serious now. Aww hell..."*

Right on cue, she erupted. Into joyous, contagious amusement. It swirled around in his head, surprising and delighting him with how just the feeling of her joy was able to lift his flagging spirits like nothing else could. Warming him to the core, like that first beam of really warm sunlight on the first day of Spring. And even though he doubted it was possible, given the place they were in, he imagined he heard it echo outside his head, and around the room as well. She slapped a hand to his chest as she continued howling.

"Okay that's it. You asked for this," he reached up and grabbed her.

"No! No! No!" She squealed, as he wrestled her down to his level. First on top of him, and then straight into the nearest man-sized dollop of ice cream.

"Hey no fair. Strawberry's your favorite. Not mine. I can't believe you did that," she sat up and slapped his arm as they smiled at each other. She looked down at herself and with a little flick of her pretty little head, she was once again clean as a whistle.

"Okay, so that just takes all the fun out of dipping you in dessert, doesn't it?"

He gave her what he hoped was his best 'I'm so into you' look.

She gave him a cheeky grin, that faltered…right into a frown.

"Yep, and you try that again and maybe next time I'll just leave you in whatever mess you find yourself, Senator. Remember that."

Okay, well, so much for that… He sighed. Definitely not the response he was going for, to say the least. Talk about crash and burn. He must be losing his touch. Of course, he was hardly at his charming best in this place.

"Duly noted." He breathed a sigh and shook off some more sticky cream from his arms, even as he mentally shelved his seduction plan for the time being. *"I'm officially jealous. You have got to show*

me how to do that popping right back to yourself thing you do."

"Maybe… And you're welcome, by the way." He heard something that sounded like an advert announcer voice with her next thought. *"All courtesy of the crazy void ice cream parlor. And please, do absolutely forget about tipping your waiter on your way out 'cause that guy is a straight-up freak."* She giggled again. *"I mean, did yuh see him?"*

So, she hadn't got there after he landed in the ice cream?

"Wait, so, you saw him? What he…uh…did to me?"

"I saw when he pushed you into the mega-bowl of ice cream, if that's what you mean."

She looked at him. Her eyes searched his for long seconds before a look of concern replaced her cheery expression. *"Oh, no… Senator…there was more, wasn't there?"*

He nodded, feeling overcome all of a sudden, he blinked away the slight wetness he felt creep into his eyes, entirely against his will, as the painful emotions of the attack came flooding back in a rush.

"I'm so sorry. It's okay. It will be okay," she tugged him forward. Pulled him into a bear hug of warmth, comfort, and surprising strength.

"Wow…that's quite a grip you've got there, Ms. Sharpe. Remind me not to mess with you." He tried to make light of it because somewhere inside, he knew he wanted her to keep holding on to him. Just like that…and never let go.

Way too soon for his liking, she released him. He shook his head and collapsed onto his back in an effort to quiet the residual shaking of his limbs.

"Hey, how'd you know strawberry's my favorite, by the way?" he glanced up at her.

"Easy. It's how they trap and torture you. They give you something they know you love, then just when you settle in and relax, they confine you. Twist it horribly in some way. Pervert it. Or just take it away entirely, so you're left sitting alone and in utter darkness in one of those awful, creepy rooms. Or worse."

"Worse?"

"Worse." Her nod plus the look on her face was both illuminating and terrifying.

"So...are we talking your basic B-rated 20th century scary, but semi-silly horror movie, or Armageddon?"

"Look, the wicked beings, lost souls...whatever they are. They're everywhere. This place is lousy with them. And as for the fallen? I think they've done nothing but study us for millennia. They are the masters of torture. Of every kind. Physical, mental, emotional. You name it. And there are no guardrails. They have free reign in here, and they are exceedingly efficient at being evil. Never doubt it. We're talking apocalyptic. Light you on fire so you can watch your own flesh melting off your bones. All while they snicker and throw sharp needles at you, and use you for dart practice, type situation. Meanwhile, and I don't even know how it could be possible, but at that very same time, somewhere in your head...you're trapped, like a caged bird. Like literally flitting back and forth, from one unimaginable, indescribable visual and sensory

horror to the next. Tailormade especially for you. What you fear. What you despise. That annoying little habit you feel like you'll never overcome, or escape. And completely unrelated to what they're subjecting your body to, by the way. So much so, that in the real world, the next morning, you wake up dizzy because they've played their freaky, twisted psychological mind games on you, for God alone knows how long. So, this place?" She waved a finger around and let out something that couldn't quite be called a laugh, *"This makes Armageddon look like a family barbecue."*

He looked away, took in a shaky breath as the gravity of her words, the horror he'd just endured, and their current surroundings all sunk in again, in an entirely new and frightening way.

"Hey." She tugged on his arm. He turned back. Met her gaze. And then watched, as her look of concern transitioned into his best-held fantasy – as she smiled. That amazing lifesaving, mind-altering, spirit-lifting smile, that was all her.

And as he liked to believe.

That was all and only for him.

"Come on now." Her pretty eyes searched his. *"I didn't mean to scare you. Just prepare you. For whatever you may have to face in here. Like I just said, it's gonna be okay. I promise. And I can say that whether I like it or not, I keep getting drawn to help you. So, we will get through this. Whatever the heck this is. Together and by the grace of God. Now, come on, don't just sit there. Freaky waiter-boy might double back. Let's go look for the light that takes us home."* She extended her hand.

He took in a deep cleansing breath, focused on her lovely face, nodded, and took her hand.

Already determined that very Sunday would be the one when he finally and whole-heartedly committed to joining a church.

Chapter 11

2 Timothy 1:7
For God hath not given us the spirit of fear; but of
power, and of love, and of a sound mind...

"So, you guys all go to the same church? Is that how you met?"

"No, we started out, all of us, on our own very personal and in some cases really weird faith walks, thanks in part to the void. Anyway, somehow, our paths all crossed in really meaningful and blessed ways. I don't know what to say, except we all sort of found each other, exactly at the time we needed to. Maybe ten years ago, and we've been best buds ever since."

"Wow, I've had some pretty freaky experiences myself of late, so I can just imagine. I can see how it could bring you together too."

"Yeah, and support or not, it can take a toll. I know. How are you coping?"

"Pretty well, I guess. All things considered. As

Rissa can attest, a fairly recent encounter with my own personal guardian angel was certainly a game-changer. It's given me a whole new perspective."

"I hear they can do that." Marly Newton shook her head with a small smile.

"Are you sure this is a good idea? I mean I shared what I found out about the defenders and their plans to target underage kids with you this afternoon because I know you. I know how many followers you have in the Underground, and you can really help get the word out. But I hadn't really planned on telling anyone else and certainly not a whole group like you've gathered today. I heard what you said, but I'm not so sure I'd be comfortable involving your friends after all. The evil I've seen scares me. What if I make myself more of a target? Open a door to even worse experiences?"

"It'll be fine, you'll see. There's nobody I trust more in the world than this group of people, and when we put our heads and praying hearts together, there's nothing we can't do. That includes stomping all over this new spiritual threat. I'll bet we can even come up with some other ways to get the word out. I'm telling you this is the right thing to do. Trust me."

"Okay." Elise relented, but wasn't entirely sure she shared her friend's optimism.

"Okay," Marly glanced over at her with a bright smile and nodded. "Right, we're here. This is Danielle and Joe's place. You're gonna love it here, trust me. Joe is just an amazing chef, and Dani, well, to say she's a riot is an understatement." She pulled into a large circular driveway. They exited her car, she grabbed her son out of his car seat in the back, and they walked up a little side path, and up to a large entryway. She waved a hand, and the door whistled open to reveal a modern-looking foyer.

"Come on in." She led the way through the living area, and then right into the kitchen where four people were gathered around a massive floating island.

"Guys, this is Elise Sharpe. She runs that great non-profit I told you about. Lise, you remember my husband Dax, right? And these are our friends, Rissa's husband – Captain Duncan Wright. And this is Lieutenant Danielle Almonzo and her husband, Dr. Joe Almonzo."

"Dax, it's been a minute, so nice to see you again. It's great to meet you all too," she shook hands all around. "Thank you so much for having me. Danielle, Joe, your house is gorgeous, by the way." She looked back towards the living area and tried not to gape at the exquisite blending of ancient and modern design.

"Aren't you sweet to say so? Thank you, Lise, just make yourself at home. Please take a seat." Danielle smiled at her warmly and pointed to a vacant comfortable looking stool on one side of the island. "Can I get you something to drink? Dax here makes a mean fruit punch."

"And I will try it, thank you."

She poured some out of a jug sitting on a chilling panel on the counter. "Here you go." She handed her a frosty glass.

"Guys, like I said this afternoon, Lise has quite a story to tell us about what Verndari are up to now. You need to hear what she has to say, and I don't think it can wait, so thanks for carving the time out of your schedules for us to get together like this. Wait, Duncan, where's Rissa?" Marly looked around. "She upstairs?"

"Oh, not here yet. She just had to finish something at work. She's picking up Peyton and they'll be here in a little while."

"Ok, good. I just need to go put Gabriel down for a nap. He's teething so he's a little fussy these days." She retrieved the adorable baby from his father's arms and rubbed his tiny back. "Dani?"

"Sure honey, you can use the kids' guest bedroom at the end of the hall. You know the way. Just turn on the AI baby monitor, she'll take care of him."

Marly nodded. "Guys…best behavior, please," she pointed around at four faces that suddenly looked wide-eyed and innocent. "We wanna make a good impression on Lise. You too Newton," she levelled a look on her husband, just before she headed up the stairs.

"What?" Dax's combination clueless yet offended expression was precious.

"I don't even know what that means." Dani shrugged and took a delicate sip from her glass just before her coms started beeping. "Guys, just give me one minute. I need to take this." She jumped off the bar stool she was sitting on and walked a bit towards the living room.

"What's up Dorran? Uh-huh… yeah… Okay… So, wait, you're saying we need to get a vehicle to get us there and back, but not be seen? Oh, I think I know someone who can help with that." She grinned.

"Okay, yeah… Leave it to me. Let me call you right back. Yeah, bye." She returned to the kitchen and approached the corner of the island where Dax was standing.

"No way Dani. Not in this lifetime, so just forget about it." He didn't even look up from what he was doing as she got near him. He kept his eyes instead on the selection of juicy and delicious looking fresh tropical fruit and bottled juices he was expertly chopping and blending.

"Come on Dax, please? We've been working on this sting operation to catch some really brazen gold smugglers in the act for weeks. We just need transport with stealth tech for the bust we're planning for tomorrow."

"So go talk to your precinct's tech gurus. Can't they hook you up with something?"

"Nothing that can allow us to take these bandits out on their turf, which as if you didn't know, is a couple thousand feet up in the air. The minimum cost of that kinda tech in a vehicle is like ten mil Newton, you know that. Since you got the first one you've been upgrading to the latest model Sky-Reacher with all the bells and whistles every time a new one comes out. Oh, and I can't speak for the other divisions, but NYPD's budget at the 15th is pretty slim. We joke all the time that it stands for **N**ot expecting **Y**'all to **P**ay a **D**ang thing." She barked out a laugh. "Duncan, back me up here. Am I lying?"

"Nope. True as the Gospel, Monzo." He shook his head on a chuckle.

"Well, that's just too bad for you guys. Sell your sad story walking, Detective. If you think I'm letting you take my precious baby, the pride and joy of my life, out on some stake-out that could potentially end in some part of it getting disintegrated by a laser weapon, or worse, you got another think coming."

"So…" The pretty hazel-hued gaze she levelled on him, turned sharp, and Lise did not envy him in the least as she anxiously waited to see what would happen next.

"Does my girl, Marly, know you consider that car to be your, what'd you just say? Oh, yeah, the precious pride and joy of your life? 'Cause I'm thinking that's something she and I are gonna need to chat about, just as soon as she gets back down those stairs."

She pursed her pretty lips and flung a handful of her glossy black curls off her shoulder, right before she put her hands on her hips, and tapped a tiny but very stylish booted foot on her porcelain floor.

He eyed her.

"Okay, so what time did you say you need it?"

"Well, dang!" She shared a look with her NYPD colleague, just before he ducked his head down to cover his grin. "Duncan? He's worse than you. Didn't think it would work that fast! Didn't even get a chance to use my best material." She laughed and clapped her hands together. "So, what'd she do to you to make you cave that quick? Dax? Come on now, you can tell Auntie Dani."

"Oh, no. Don't do that. Don't bring that voice you use with the kids into this. Let's just say I nearly lost an earlobe a while ago, for a far more menial infraction, and with a promise to, and I quote, "grab a hold of something that will hurt a whole lot more" should there ever be a repeat."

"Ooowee!" Dani made a hissing sound.

"Wow," Duncan winced.

"Didn't know my girl had it in her. It's always the quiet looking ones that got a little of that crazy fire, huh?" Dani wondered.

"You have no idea."

"So anyway, around nine-ish tomorrow night work for you?"

"I'll be here. Joe, I expect you'll have a double portion of my favorite seafood risotto waiting?"

"Consider it done. I got you buddy. We'll make a night of it. Duncan?"

"Oh yeah, boys' night in? We haven't had one of those in a while. Great timing too. I gotta take care of Peyton. Rissa's working late tomorrow. Prob'ly pulling an all-nighter with her clients' usual month end deadlines, so sure, I wouldn't miss it for the world."

"Okay great, I'll tell the twins. They always love it when you bring him for a sleep over." Joe smiled.

"Dani, I'm serious though. If you or Dorran put so much as the tiniest scratch on that car… I swear by all that's holy–"

"Yeah, yeah. Take it easy. We'll be super careful. Besides, even if it were to meet with a little mishap, I'm sure the department will pay to fix and or replace it. In the circumstances."

"Really?"

"Of course not," she snorted. "Did you just completely miss the part where I told you how broke we are? Doubt I could get them to pony up enough dough for a cup of coffee, and you think they could fix a car worth like what? A cool sixteen mil? Get outta here." She slapped him on the back and giggled.

"Really?" He turned to Joe. "You gonna let her do me like that? A fellow brother in the faith? Don't you have anything to say?"

"None yuh." Joe uttered the simple phrase without even looking up from his cutting board, and his near surgical slicing of a variety of brightly colored vegetables.

"Excuse me?"

He put down his knife then, his gorgeous gray-blue gaze swung towards Dax. "I sleep in the same room behind closed doors with this woman, and I intend on doing exactly *nothing* that will ever jeopardize what goes on behind said doors. EVER. And as far as that goes, well that's 'none yuh' business, so you're on your own brother. 'Nough said."

"I heard that." Duncan bumped fists with him as he chuckled. Joe turned to his wife. "Isn't that right, sweet pea?" He leaned down. Dani plunged her fingers into the rich waves of his salt and pepper hair, and gave him a kiss that would have made a sinner blush. Then she whispered something in his ear, right before he went back to chopping his vegetables, with a secret little smile plastered across his handsome face.

"That's my man, right there." Dani grinned at Lise, looked at Dax, and then burst into laughter.

"Seriously? Not cool guys." Dax shook his head.

Reminded of the always entertaining, sometimes slightly inappropriate banter she so often shared with

Chaz; Elise returned Dani's grin.

No longer fearful about sharing her secret with so many because suddenly, she felt right at home.

Chapter 12

Romans 1:20
For the invisible things of Him from the creation of the
world are clearly seen, being understood by the things
that are made, even His eternal power and Godhead; so
that they are without excuse...

It was a beautiful day to visit the Eiffel Tower.

No longer fearful of the height, Elise stepped out of the elevator on the highest floor. It had taken a while, but she was finally getting the hang of these dream treks of hers. Expanding her horizons was turning out to be fear-crushing and enriching. Both spiritually uplifting, and emotionally therapeutic.

"Woah!" She grasped the railing to steady herself as a sudden gust of wind threatened to topple her. The tour director had just said to be careful because of how windy it could be at this higher altitude. He certainly wasn't kidding.

It was all worth it for the view of course. The Seine directly below, the amazing city of Paris spread out all around, and straight ahead, nothing but gorgeous blue sky. She really had to give Kai props for this particular D.I.E.T. He was getting better and better at tailoring the intensity and variety of the experiences to suit her tastes, and her capacity for mental growth. Without a doubt he rocked! And he'd truly outdone himself this time.

She looked around to express her gratitude, but didn't see any sign of him. That was strange… he was normally fairly nearby.

"Oh, he's not here this time."

"Excuse me?" She spun at the sound of the voice behind her. Saw no one at her eye level, until she looked down.

"He's not here, but I am!" A mannish face, on the body of a seven-year-old child was leering up at her. Hissed at her like a serpent, as he lurched forward, his face transforming into a hideous beast with scary black eyes and fangs. She screamed and took a hasty step back.

Right off the Eiffel Tower. And into thin air.

She tried to fly, as she'd done in the void a thousand times, but just couldn't. Instead, every fear, every phobia she'd ever experienced surrounding heights came rushing back. In a cascade of throat-closing, chest-squeezing, breath-stopping terror.

Her field of vision dimmed. Her world was growing smaller. Closing in, and rushing up to meet her, all at the same time. She was about to plunge to her death, directly into the Seine. And it would be like hitting concrete from this high up, she knew. An urgent prayer had barely crossed her lips when out of nowhere, she was caught up and held in strong arms.

"Oh God! Oh God!" she screamed, feeling like

her heart was going to explode in her chest as she gripped her rescuer's neck.

"It's okay. You're okay now. Breathe Lise, just breathe." Kai stroked her hair and her back with a soothing touch as they safely and softly touched down to earth.

"That felt so real. They got me and I didn't even know it. Why didn't I know it?"

Normally she had a sense of her surroundings changing whenever she found herself in the void. But this time, she didn't have so much as a clue.

He set her down gently, right into her seat at their favorite table at that little outdoor café in Nice. Waited. Allowed her the minute or two it took for her to feel comfortable enough to let go. To release the strangle hold she had on his neck.

"Okay?" He gave her hand a little squeeze when she finally focused on him and leaned back in her chair.

Her nod felt jerky. With her shaking as much as she was.

"So, I got you some of your fave pastries. Look good, huh? No? Aww come on Lise. Talk to me, please?"

"I'm not in the mood for any dang pastries, okay?" She reached out. Fought for control to stop the seemingly uncontrollable trembling that had set into her limbs. Shoved the plate away. And watched in amazement, as it disintegrated into star dust, and blew away on a soft breeze.

Stunned, she looked across the table.

Allowed herself to be drawn into his precious blue gaze. Encircled and held. It was like she'd just taken another dive. But this time into comfort and compassion. Into serenity and warmth. Feeling better almost instantly, she took a deep breath, and soaked in his calming presence. Full measure.

"Besides," she shrugged, "that kind of excess is fine once in a while. Anything more, like when you start to live for it. Make it some kind of idol," she shook her head. "Even in this dream realm, that becomes greed, and that's a sin… You know that."

"I do." His smile was aptly angelic.

"Okay, so score one for the good team. Another lesson learned. The evils of gluttony. Check. Thank you. I guess," she shrugged again.

"This is not about keeping score Lise. It's about choices, and you're the only one who can make them. Remember? Unfortunately, there's the delightful, the good, the bad and–"

"And let me guess…the really freakin' ugly?"

"Not my words, but yes. You meet it all, along the way on your journey."

"Oh, well check and check on the last two." She'd just had her fill of the really bad and the really ugly. All at once, that was for sure.

"You take from this what you will. Every time."

"Yeah, I know. And I'm sorry. You rescued me and did all this," she waved a hand over the now empty table, "I didn't mean to sound ungrateful. It's just that I feel like such a fraud, telling the senator just the other night I'll help him through things like what just happened to me, and I can't even rescue myself. These attacks are getting scarier and more real. It's getting so I'm not sure if I'm asleep, or awake anymore. I just don't know if I can do this.

Any of this. Maybe I'm not strong enough." She took in a ragged breath.

"Hey…hey now. Look at me." He urged her gaze to his with a gentle finger beneath her chin. "Yes, you can. And yes, you absolutely are strong enough. Because He is. Come on now, do you think I could do any of what I do without Him?"

"And that's great for you. You're an angel, Kai. Whereas I… Well…I'm just me," she shrugged.

"Just you? Are you kidding me? You, my dearest Elise Madeline Sharpe, are the beloved! Crowned with glory and honor. From the very foundation of time, you were chosen. And I don't mean that 'you' in the general sense of your humanity, I mean you specifically. He numbers the hairs on your head Lise. Do you know how amazing that is?! To be loved like that? Unconditionally, completely, without reservation, or need for reciprocation? I do. And so do you. *If* you stop and think about it. Put yourself at the center of His will and just *feel* His awesome power."

As he spoke, the atmosphere around them changed. It became charged, with what she couldn't say. Day turned into night, and she looked up, as the skies above them rapidly darkened. Overhead, hazy purple gases began combining out of nothingness. Colliding. Swirling and then exploding, with millions of pinpoints of light. All across the vastness of space. And she realized intuitively, she'd just had a front row seat, to the formation of an entirely new galaxy.

"Oh my God… that was amazing! To say incredible doesn't even cover it. Wow… Did you see that?" Breathless, she looked back at Kai.

"All the time. Welcome to my world Lise." His smile was more radiant than she'd ever seen it. Maybe because this time the aura of light that so often wreathed him, pulsed in perfect harmony with the life throbbing within the brand-new heavenly creation she'd just seen formed out of thin air, high overhead.

"And you're a part of it too. We all are. You only have to believe, and you *will* know, that the One who can do *that*, will not hesitate. EVER. To move heaven and earth…for you."

And in that moment, she knew she was loved. Like never before.

And she knew, no other words about it were, or would ever be necessary.

Ever again.

Chapter 12

1 John 2:16
For all that is in the world, the lust of the flesh, and the
lust of the eyes, and the pride of life, is not of the Father,
but is of the world...

"*Oh, you've got* to be kidding me. *Again?*"

She grabbed the senator's hand and pulled him through and then out of some kind of ginormous sticky mess he was trying desperately to escape.

"*I'd explain, but it kinda feels like there are no words for just how bad that experience you just saved me from really was.*"

"*Yeah, no words necessary. But I have to ask. What's with you and all this food anyway? And desserts in particular. What is it this time? Pumpkin pie?*"

She flew them to a quiet spot at the very center of the outdoor maze she'd entered to save him. Settled, then helped him get most of the sticky goop off his head and face with the water from the gentle gurgling fountain next to where they were sitting.

"It's sweet potato actually." She heard the gravelly, if somewhat weary tone of his voice in her head. *"And if you must know…it happens to be my favorite."*

"Well, not anymore, after this episode, I'm guessing."

He sighed and shook some pastry off his arm.

"Yuh know, you must be the second unluckiest person in the great state of New York to keep ending up in this kinda trouble in here."

"I know, right? Wait. Did you say second unluckiest, though? Who's the first?"

"Oh, you're looking at her."

"HA! I seriously doubt you've seen the things I have, Ms. Sharpe. You have no idea what I've been through lately. I'm almost positive I've got you beat."

"Oh, really? Well, let's measure freaky experiences, shall we? Like for instance, tonight, right before I got drawn here to help you, I was on a plane. A place in the void I'm pretty certain I've never been before, but the fallen still manage to make it feel eerily familiar somehow.

"Well… At first.

"You know? Like you've been there a million times and you've known the people you see all your life. So, there we all are, some sitting facing each other, some standing around, and just shooting the breeze. The narrator of this entire horror show, who I can't see, speaks softly near my left ear, introducing everyone by name. "Remember so-and-so," she says, and I nod and smile, although I know I really don't. In fact, I have absolutely no clue who any of them

might be, let alone what their names are. Still, I have this nagging sense that we've all met before, so I play along, politely pretending I know the next name she speaks, and the one after that.

"Across from me is a woman I feel sure is a friend. She's always in these elaborate designer dresses. Wants to be admired and applauded for her latest creations. She twists and turns, twirling like a child across the aisle from me. Then she comes over to where I'm sitting, invites me to touch the fabric of the outfit she's modeling, to see how lovely it is. "Brava," I say to her and clap my hands together, as though praising her like that is something I do every day. Though I'm pretty sure I've never said that particular word before, in my entire life."

"Brava? Really? You sure that's what you said?"

"Yes! My point exactly. Who in the world even says that, right? Then, there's the grinning caricature of someone who looks vaguely like one of my girlfriends. She and her husband, pop in from first class. She's weirdly disfigured and he's tiny. I mean he's doll-sized. Like no more than a foot tall and five pounds at most, and yet I don't even bat an eye. For some reason this strikes me as being perfectly normal. They glare at me for no good reason then go back through the door to the front of the plane.

"Next, that silent, handsome, arrogant man I just know I should remember, rises from his seat on the right and smirks as he comes over to me. He thrusts his Armani covered hips forward, sticks his crotch right in my face and shrugs with a smile, as

though I'd do whatever he wants. Like I can't help but comply, just because he's rich and attractive. 'Not today G-money,' I giggle and swat him away like I know I do every single time, so I won't hurt his feelings too much. While inside, I wanna kick him. Hard. And scream at him, As if! Not even if you were the last man on earth. I mean, NEVER in this lifetime, or even the next one, buddy!

"*Oh, then there's the woman to the left. I can never really see who she is, but she is hands-down the cheer director of the group. I mean, funny and sounding so happy, but then every now and again this strange overwhelming feeling emanates from her in flashes and disturbing waves. It's hard to describe, but I just know she's hiding such a deep, dark sadness behind all that cheer.*

"*And then out of the blue, it hits me. She…is me. The pretending to be fine when I'm not. The soul crushing energy it takes to put on a brave face for the world, all the time, so everyone around me can continue on with their lives, not giving me another thought.*

"*In fact, all of those women. They were all me. All the darkest aspects of my personality. Right there on hideous display. All the different terrible things I labor so hard to hide every single day. Sure, they inspire sin, the fallen ones, but no one ever tells you how well they mirror it. Like you wouldn't believe. And trust me, they are in their element, when you're at your very worst. Never doubt it.*

"*Oh, I'd love to be able to blame them, but that right there, yeah…that was all me. All the sinful things I shamefully sometimes wish I could be to get* *along, and fit in, to please the world. Right there in front of me, and all around. Because yes, sometimes I do long to have someone stroke my ego and be seen and admired like the woman in the dress. To walk into a room and be the **only** one anybody notices. Or to have a husband like my friend. To be counted among the chosen. Chosen. By any man, however unsuited he may be for me. No matter how bad the marriage. If I'm honest, somewhere deep inside I still envy every woman I meet who's attained that coveted state of union, and that grand title of wife because my chance to wear that title was stripped away from me. When I least expected it..."*

"But not his ring?"

His soft question pulled her from her bitter remembrance, right back to their shadowy present. *"Huh?"*

"You still wear his ring." He lifted and fingered the band that swung at her chest. *"He gave this to you, didn't he? The man who hurt you?"*

"No. Danny didn't hurt me. Why would you say that?" Confused, she pulled the ring from his loose grasp. *"He loved me. We were going to be married, but he was killed in a car crash."*

"Oh, darn it. I'm so sorry. I shouldn't have said that. I didn't know."

"No. It's fine. How would you? It was a long time ago anyway. I just haven't been able to bring myself to stop wearing it. Just another example of me pretending to be something I'm not, I suppose. Because maybe, just maybe, someone seeing it would think I'm married, and just like that, suddenly I'm among the chosen. Hey, in the club by mistaken

assumption is still better than not at all."

She took a bracing pause.

"It's a humbling and sobering moment, when you learn that all on your own, you could be far worse and more terrifying than anything in this place."

"So, you think you're all those women." The senator's voice in her head was low, and softer than she'd ever heard it. *"But, what about the disrespectful man?"*

"What? Can't you guess?" She tried, but couldn't quite meet his gaze, as he slowly shook his head. Thought about trying a laugh. Unsure she wanted to reveal even more of herself to him, she faltered. Took in a deep breath instead. *"Well, I've come this far, so you might as well know. That too, Senator, is me."*

He looked surprised. Shocked even, at her response.

"Yep. Welcome to the world of envious me. The one who wishes she had the freedom and privileges afforded to every man on this planet. To bend everyone to their will, as they talk over me, dismissing my point of view and labeling it as agreeing to disagree. To be able to take a strong, principled position anywhere, any time, and not be branded the head, you-know-what, in charge in the room, as people tend to do with women, but never men. To command a higher wage for doing exactly the same job as a woman. Hell, to screw everything that moves, and be called experienced, and be admired even, rather than being trotted out as a whore."

His brows rose above wide gray eyes, and she wondered if that right there was the proverbial bridge too far.

Well…too late now…

"Anyway, the atmosphere changed after that." She forced her mind to revisit the conclusion of her macabre story. *"Fear entered the room. In a big way. You've felt what that's like in here, haven't you?"*

He nodded.

"Alive. Shadowy. Choking. I'm talking just mind-numbing terror. Like a living thing it blankets me, gripping me, till I can't even think, or move. Yet still so familiar, like an old, really cruel family member, or an entrenched addiction. And just when I think I can't stand another second—

"Yes…that's right…just give up. It's too late for you," the narrator snarls in my ear, right before they all disappear like a puff of smoke. And like a scene from a mind-bending movie, the lines and angles of the walls all around me begin to change, as section by section, the room rapidly collapses in on itself. It gets dark, so dark…and I think this is it, I'm done for. But then, I see it. Way off to the left. To the farthest corner, where instead of closing doors and spaces… This one is opening.*

"Light begins seeping in. First just in a small puddle on the floor, and then in a bright white cascade, it moves forward…at the speed of footsteps, to obliterate every speck of darkness… from ceiling to floor. And before I can see Him, I'm jolted into yet another reality. This one. But with a prayer lingering in my head. One I don't even remember saying. The one that saved me. The one that always saves me.

*Releasing me from the prison of my mind – Thank you Lord, for lighting **all** my dark places."*

She looked up at the gloomy sky overhead then closed her eyes for a moment, reliving the pure power of those Holy Spirit gifted words. She took another deep breath.

"So, there you have it. Bet you can't top that, huh? A spectacular rescue at the end sure, but still a really chilling encounter with my secret shame."

Feeling suddenly chilled, she rubbed her arms. *"I gotta get outta here. I swear, this place acts like my own personal truth serum. I feel like I can say and do just about anything in here. I guess because just about everything has happened to me."* She tried a dry laugh. *"Can't even imagine what you must think of me now. After hearing all that."* She shook her head. Looked down at her bare feet for a moment. And wondered…if she'd truly said too much.

Expecting a comment of censure, or a really awkward silence, instead, she felt the gentle nudge of his finger beneath her chin. Drawing her gaze back to his.

"I think what I've always thought. That you are a bright, beautiful, and incredibly amazing woman."

His gray regard enveloped her. Crept into all her empty places, filling them with his particular brand of intriguing illumination. As only he could.

"Well…all except for your hair. Sorta looks like mine tonight. Kinda kooky actually. Not cute. At all, by the way."

"Really?"

"Hey, you asked."

A giggle escaped her at the adorable grin on his

face.

"Ah...there it is, the smile that rocks my world. Every time."

She rolled her eyes.

*"I'm not kidding. You don't even recognize your own appeal. Do you? And just so you know, we all have moments where we fail miserably at being **in** the world, but not **of** it. And FYI, having confidence in your ability...in yourself, is not arrogance. There's a marked difference. Even if you don't fully believe it, I hope what I said resonates with you, to some degree at least."*

"Enough. For now..." She nodded.

"Good." He looked up and around. *"I still don't understand any of this, I don't mind saying. I've been praying more, as I'm sure you've been. I see you at church every Sunday."*

"Really? I didn't know you'd joined. Good for you! But I haven't even caught a glimpse of you. Not one time, and you've seen me? How is that even possible?"

"Oh, it's not so surprising. I tend to sit in the newly repentant sinners' section at the back. Not up near the front with the seasoned righteous regulars like yourself." His quirky smile widened as she gasped.

"Oh my God...you did not just seat-shame me like that."

"Hey, I just call it, like I see it." He grinned.

"Yeah, okay, well try coming over to say hi some time, Newly Repentant."

"Okay... Maybe I will... and why do I feel like that name's gonna stick?"

"Hey, you said it. I didn't." She returned his grin.

"Seriously though, I keep thinking I'm making real progress, but it just doesn't seem to be helping with these attacks. Not sure what else to call them, or make of them."

"Neither do I, but just keep doing what you're doing. Remember what the reverend said just last week – that sometimes, strange spiritual attacks seem to come at you, and even get worse the closer you get to your breakthrough?"

"Oh, yeah. I remember. Well, if that's the case, I'm expecting a holy ghost miracle like you wouldn't believe. Any day now, given what I've been through in the last couple months."

"I hear you."

"Come on." He stood. Took her hand in a warm grasp. Tugged her to her feet. *"The light will be here soon and you promised to show me how to fly like you do."*

"Okay, sure."

She smiled, joined her mind with his and looked up into the night sky.

Thrilled, by his joyful shout in her head, she propelled them both high up into the air at superspeed.

Chapter 13

Matthew 13:45-46
Again, the kingdom of heaven is like unto a merchant
man, seeking goodly pearls: Who, when he had found
one pearl of great price, went and sold all that he had,
and bought it...

"Hey Lise."

"Hey Kai. You finally gonna give in tonight and show me how to fly like you do? You know, that snappy-fingers thing you do?"

"Sorry, angel-privilege." He grinned.

"Figures." She pursed her lips to show him her displeasure. "So, then where are we going tonight?" Excited for the trek ahead, she clapped then rubbed her hands together, as she looked around at the really well-appointed room in which they were sitting.

"At the moment, the Executive Suite at Garringdown's, in Mayfair."

"Whoa... London, huh? Fancy... I could get used to this." She rose from her chair and took a little walk through the suite with Kai trailing behind her in silence.

Everywhere she looked, the space just oozed sophistication and regal elegance, with its super expensive looking furnishings, and finely detailed historical accents.

"So, we got time to raid the minibar?" She turned to him and grinned.

"Now, why did I just know you were gonna ask that?" He barked out a laugh. "Does this place look like it would have a minibar, to you?"

"Hey, how would I know?" She shrugged.

"No. No minibar. Try on-call, round-the-clock, butler service."

"Wow. For real?"

He nodded.

"That's impressive. I've read about places like this. Never thought I'd ever get to visit one though."

"I know. So, what do you think?"

"I think I might not be as comfortable here as I imagined I would."

"Really? Why's that?"

She pointed to one of a few antique vases artfully positioned around the ultra-exquisite lounge. It was resting on an equally ancient-looking table. "What does that cost? I'd be afraid I might break the dang thing, every minute I spent in here. Even *if* I could afford to replace it."

"Interesting perspective and very practical." He chuckled.

"Yuh know, every now and again I get that 'I'm not enough, don't have enough, or I haven't done well enough,' feeling. Haven't gotten my standard minutes of fame that everyone's fighting for these days. And here I am, standing in one of *the* most opulent places in all of London. If this was in the real world? I don't think I'd be taking dozens of selfies to post on social media because all I can think is, it must really be kind of a downer. Yuh know? To aspire to get here. To spend so much money on a fancy place like this, so you'd be seen. Only to find you'd be just as happy, or maybe even happier at one of those new comfy, inexpensive boutique motels, with the premium food synthesizers. It's like you said, I think maybe I already have all I'll ever need, and fame isn't what it's cracked up to be either."

She paused as she pondered that little revelation.

"Wait…is there another lesson in there somewhere for me?"

"Hey, I'm just providing the fantasy." Kai held up his hands in a gesture of surrender. "You can take from it what you will. Remember?"

"Uh-huh," she eyed him. "Still, think I've been played though, but okay."

She didn't say anything else, but judging by the slight knowing smile on his face, she knew she was right. She wasn't sure exactly when, but at some point, all the experiences she'd been having, good and bad, were becoming increasingly more cathartic. Still freaky as all hell, some of them. But absolutely more purposeful, she guessed was the best way to describe them. Unbidden, the senator came to her mind, and she hoped that in some small way, he was coming to that same beneficial conclusion too, with his nightly trials.

"Okay, come on, I'd say you've seen enough. We gotta go meet Raphael and Archie now." He waved a hand over a shining panel on the nearby wall, and it opened the doors to an elevator.

"Very nice." She stepped in ahead of him and took a seat on one of the padded benches that lined the walls.

"Is this really necessary?" She tapped the bands of light that unfurled over her shoulders and down her chest, then intersected with the one in her lap as the doors closed, cocooning them in luxurious, dimly lit silence. "These energy restraints?"

"Oh yeah, definitely, and I'd suggest you hang on to them too, and get ready."

"Get ready? For what? The ride to the ground floor?" She snorted.

"No. For this." He grinned.

No sooner were the words out of his mouth than her world shifted. Literally. Both the elevator and the bench they were on tilted sharply to the side, swung to face the opposite direction, dropped down again and then shot forward and upward, at a rate that pressed her right up against the back of the seat. For sure, this is what it must have felt like to be shot out of a cannon she figured, as she heard Kai's joyous laughter, while screaming at the top of her lungs.

And she enjoyed every minute of it!

Suddenly, the elevator rapidly transformed into a scenic one, made entirely of plexiglass. Allowing her picturesque glimpses of the city below through its transparent sides and floor, as they whizzed by overhead. Big Ben, the river Thames, the Tower of London, Buckingham Palace, the London Eye, all set against the backdrop of a lingering sunset. Everything she'd ever imagined and more, shown off in spectacular fashion in the fading early evening light.

Kai looked down and pointed. "Okay, here we are at the next stop on tonight's multiple venue sightseeing trip."

"For real?" She couldn't wait to see what else he had in store for them.

"Absolutely. Are you ready?"

"You know I am. Bring it on!"

Their ride took a steep dive and before she knew it, they'd come to a sliding stop on the sidewalk she'd just spotted through her window to the world.

"My lady," he extended his hand to help her exit their transport. "Welcome to the world of wax…and light."

"No way…" She looked around and sure enough there was the street sign on the corner. "Marylebone Road?" With a flourish, Kai indicated the sign above her head on the wall.

"Madame Tussauds? Are you kidding me?!" Elise was beside herself with excitement.

"I've wanted to come here since I was a kid." She turned to Kai, "Now this…this is awesome! The best trip yet. I owe you one Kai."

"Think nothing of it. All part of the experience."

"So, is she just loving it, or what?"

"Even more than you thought." Kai bumped fists with Raphie who'd just strolled over with Archie to join them.

"Told yuh."

"Yeah, you called it all right."

They all joined the short line going into the museum.

Archie looked up as a sudden laser light-show started directly overhead as soon as they stepped inside the first chamber. "Aren't we here to discuss next steps to stall the new bill going to the house for the defenders' implant your kid campaign? Seems to me we'd want to do that somewhere less crowded," he glanced around as he frowned, "and quiet."

"Oh, poo. Don't be such a kill-joy Archie." She grasped his arm to urge him along. "We can do both just fine. We'll have our little discussion as we walk through, and while I get a chance to enjoy this ground-breaking, award-winning integration of wax, lasers, and nanotech," she waved her hand around, beamed, and then posed like a 21st century game show model.

He didn't look convinced.

"What? Can't do two things at once? Is that it? Yuh know, you should probably try taking a meeting while doing something else, like…uh…skiing for instance. I understand it works wonders for honing your multi-tasking skills. The world is getting more challenging by the day, yuh know. Yuh gotta at least try to keep up."

"What?" The sharp look he gave her, plus his high-pitched response spoke volumes. He'd obviously never gone skiing in his life.

"Okay, so maybe not skiing. How about while playing tennis then?" She took in his pot-bellied, less than athletic looking physique, "or maybe while golfing? Yeah, that looks more your…uh…speed. I guess…"

"Okay… Good talk." He turned away from her towards the angels. Both of whom had curious looks on their faces as they followed the ongoing exchange.

"Raphie? What's the next phase of the plan?"

"Okay," the archangel regarded them both for a moment more then launched right in, "any offensive we plan has to include the parents, if it has any chance of succeeding. So, petitions, neighborhood rallies, email, physical outreach, church meetings, keep using the Underground." He checked off each item on a different finger. "Whatever you can do to galvanize the population into action and get them on the side of what's right. Both of you," he turned to her.

They carried on their little strategy session quite successfully after that, as they walked through all the ancient and modern sections of the world-famous museum.

Leading their little group, she started the trek down a nearby antique staircase that led back to the ground floor and the exit, once they'd finished seeing the planetarium and the Chamber of Horrors. Intrigued, she spun to follow the nearby arc of a random laser beam that was zipping around the space causing mixed alarm and delight by the sound of it.

"Oh!" It brushed the length of her arm like a lover's caress setting off a cascade of unexpected sensations, and she completely lost her footing. This time her cry was one of fear as she anticipated an unpleasant tumble down the short flight of stairs. But it was not to be, as strong, even if slightly clammy hands, grasped and steadied her.

"You, okay?" Archie's kind brown gaze searched hers.

"Uh, yeah. Thanks."

"You should probably keep a hold of the railing there," he pointed to the brassy looking antique.

"Right, thanks." She grasped the safety barrier as he advised, started her descent, then glanced back.

Well, that was surprising…

"Okay guys." Kai's voice broke into her musings as soon as they all got to the ground floor. "Let's take this discussion on the road. Next stop – to Versailles we go."

"Really? Yay!" She clapped her hands together and grinned as she received Kai's nod and smile. Dismissing her recent scare and the feelings her unexpected rescue elicited, she felt a swift return of eager excitement at the prospect of visiting another iconic venue on her bucket list. "Item number twenty-two! Can you believe it?" She felt like a kid at Christmas.

"What?" She noticed Archie's thoughtful look.

"Nothing." He shook his head.

"Come on, you're gonna love it! I keep telling you, yuh gotta live a little Archie, and what better way to do that, than at Versailles!" Arms outstretched, she twirled like a ballerina again and beamed at him. This time she thought his little smile actually reached his eyes.

They exited the museum and then they all piled into the elevator that appeared like magic on the sidewalk. They got to their next destination in a fairly short time and started walking towards the entrance.

"So, I guess this is what heaven must be like, huh? The gates? The golden streets and the shiny new city of Jerusalem?" Elise had to remember to close her mouth as she gaped at the gold-plated barrier as they walked through the massive entryway with scores of other people.

Kai and Raphie looked at her, and then at each other, and burst into loud and joyous laughter.

"What? What's so funny?"

Kai sobered. "Oh, wait…you're being serious right now?"

"Yeah, of course I am. It's an honest question."

"Okay, so simple answer. No."

"Really? Not even a little bit?"

"Nope. Not even a nanocyte."

"To quote you… Hell no." Raphie chimed in. "And I can say that because, well…you get it." He and Kai shared a laugh.

"Oh…okay. So, care to elaborate on how it's different then?" She hoped she'd skillfully maneuvered them into revealing at least a little something.

"Nice try." Kai grinned at her.

"Aww come on guys. We just want a little hint. Right Archie?"

"Absolutely. I'd be crazy to say no."

"See? You can give us just a little sneaky peek into heaven, can't you? Pleeease."

"Okay, sure." Kai looked to Raphie and he nodded.

"Yay!" She yelled, then got quiet and leaned in so she wouldn't miss a word.

"The kingdom of heaven is like the one who soweth good seed. The treasure found to surpass all treasures. The grain of mustard seed that once grown, is the greatest of them all."

"Yeah, yeah. I know all that. I mean I've read that already. But what's it *really* like."

"Well, if you've read it, then all you *really* need to know is, it is *He*… He who makes all things new." Kai offered with a serene smile.

"Wow. You know, you said that just then, and it's like I could sense…something. I can't explain it. It was like a flash. Something that felt really amazing, and then it was gone. You…the two of you, you're accustomed to being in His actual presence. I can't even dream of what that must be like. But dear God…what's it like when you have to leave? To step out of heaven and come be with us on earth? I mean, how can you even stand it?" She addressed Kai, then turned to Raphie, "Being away from Him, at all?"

"I'm not sure how to explain it, so that you would understand," Raphie ventured with a soft smile, "except to say, we are never apart. Distance in prayer and worship is no distance at all. It is the very same for you, beloved. Even now… You are in His very presence. If only you would just believe it…"

He reached out. Gently caressed her face with such love and reverence, she had to blink away sudden tears.

"Kai, me, our entire brotherhood, we are all messengers of the Most High. We serve at the pleasure of our King. It is quite simply what we were made for. We go where and when we are needed. We do only and exactly what we are meant to do. And make no mistake, it is our supreme pleasure, and our greatest joy. Always and forever. Amen?" He turned to his brother in arms with a brilliant smile.

"Like you wouldn't believe."

They bumped fists. And where their knuckles met, was an explosion of light. Unlike anything she'd ever seen. Their faces went from merely glowing, to reflecting transcendent luminescence. A light that was a million times brighter than the shiny castle gates they'd all just walked through.

"Wow," both she and Archie said at the same time. They looked at each other and smiled.

"I'd say that says it all, wouldn't you?" Archie ventured.

"All I ever needed to know," she nodded, in wholehearted agreement.

Chapter 14

James 4:7
Submit yourselves therefore to God. Resist the devil, and he will flee from you...

"So, you see, you don't need to do this. Any of you." Gratified, Elise watched as one or two members of her impromptu audience nodded and even responded in wholehearted agreement with her impassioned argument.

It was lunchtime and while passing by, on the other side of the street, she'd noticed a small group of people awaiting their turn to enter one of the Verndari implantation centers. Unable to just stand by and watch as they damned their eternal souls, she crossed the street and struck up a conversation. Relying entirely on the leading of the Spirit, she employed a combination of logic, basic economics, biblical lessons, and a healthy dose of good old fashioned moral suasion. And before she knew it, she'd started winning them over, one by one.

She looked around again at each of the couple

dozen faces in the small group gathered around her and saw at least one she recognized. She remembered him because of how gorgeous he was, and articulate. Despite his somewhat dirty and disheveled appearance, his clothes looked like they'd once been finely tailored. Each time she'd seen him she'd always wondered what his story was, and how a beautiful black man like him could have fallen on such hard times.

"Stuart?"

He looked surprised, but nodded slowly.

"It's me Elise. You've been to the shelter down the street. Haven't you? A couple months ago, right? Hi! I remember you. Please, tell them. We have room, for anyone who needs a place to stay, and a great team of dedicated people to take care of them. And for those who just need some food, we have groceries, enough for them and their families." She nodded at him and smiled in encouragement.

"Uh…yeah," looking hesitant he nodded as he turned to face the people next to and behind him. "She's telling the truth. I've been there and they helped me out when things went really bad for me."

"See? And since then, we've gotten a lot more funding. I know many of you are facing hardships I can't even imagine, but–"

"Yeah, you can't. You in your fancy clothes." An angry voice called out. "What you're talking about is just temporary. This, what the defenders are offering, is permanent. What are we supposed to do when the food you give us runs out, huh?"

"I'm glad you asked that because we've recently partnered with certain agencies that can help find you jobs. Also, until you get a position, what with the additional funding we received, we can provide you with supplies that will last you months instead of just days."

A chorus of interested sounds, and surprised approval rose up from the group. Riding on the positive response, she moved to close the deal.

"So, please come. Just come with me. All of you. Right now. The shelter I mentioned, it's right down the street, just there." She pointed. "It's lunchtime so you'll be able to sit and enjoy a nice, hot meal, and then as soon as you've eaten, if you'd like, you can collect some groceries, toiletries, and even a few medical supplies you might like to take home to your families. All that you can carry now. At least enough for a couple days, and we'll arrange to get the rest to you within the week. I promise, you won't regret it. Certainly not like you definitely will if you make the decision to go into that building and change your life in ways you can't even imagine. Permanently."

"Hey! You there, what do you think you're doing?" An impossibly large man, obviously a defender, judging by his black beady eyes strode through the now open center doors and out onto the sidewalk. He walked over, and like the red sea, the small group parted so he could get to her. "Move along before I have you escorted from the property."

She'd only ever seen them on her social media feeds. People always said they were huge and intimidating, but faced with a live one, standing just a short distance away, she had to admit that description didn't really do this particular menacing individual justice.

Terrified, she squared her shoulders and prayed for guidance as she prepared to do battle for the souls of the people gathered, if necessary.

"I'm conducting a one-woman peaceful protest, if you must know. And by the way, last I checked this was a free country. Much like this sidewalk, which I believe is open to the public. So, if I want to stand here and talk to these people all day long, legally, there's not a dang thing you can do about it. And that is precisely what I intend to do. If I have to, actually. Anything to stop them from entering that building because what you're doing in there is wrong and evil. You know it, and so do I." She levelled a gaze on him that she knew would leave him in no doubt as to exactly to what knowledge she was referring.

He took a single threatening step towards her, and somewhere in her mind she registered the urgent need to flee. However, she froze instead, a scream beginning to form in her throat, when–

"Bro, if you don't back up off the lady right now… you and I? Oh, we about to have a serious problem!"

She spun at the sound of Chaz's deep-throated shout. Never quite so happy and relieved to see him, she watched as, bag in hand, he dodged a taxicab like a quarterback at a game that had just gone into overtime, as he dashed across the street to get to her.

"Really?" He looked down at her and grinned when he reached her in record time. "I leave you for like ten minutes to get us lunch, and come out to find you about to get a beat down from some butt ugly Verndari?"

"Uh, you know me, I like to live on the wild side.

Next time how about I go in and get the sandwiches instead, huh?"

"I think that would be best. Well, provided I live through this." Brows nearly up to his hairline he took in a deep breath, handed her the bag, and gently urged her to stand to his side. "Don't suppose any of your new friends will help me out?" he said in a low tone for her ears only.

They both turned back, only to realize the little group was dispersing, rapidly. In about ten seconds flat there was no one left on that section of the curb but them and the defender. He leered at them and started to walk forward.

"I'm guessing not."

"Yeah, that figures. Okay, let's get this over with." He rocked his head from side to side as the defender approached him. His face set in fierce determination, his chin popped up for a second in the guy's direction. "What's up?"

Suddenly the center doors whistled open and to her surprise and great pleasure Kai strode out. Unhurried and looking like the champion he was. Strong. Wreathed in all the power and glory of the Almighty. And not dressed quite as casual as usual. He'd ditched his habitual T-shirt and jeans for a soft white shirt and khaki slacks, and his hair, normally free flowing, was pulled back in a very masculine ponytail. In short, he looked every bit as tall, hunky, and gorgeous as she remembered.

From the night before.

He walked right up to them. Nodded at her and Chase with a slight smile. Then he turned and addressed the defender.

"You're done here."

Just three little words, spoken in a deceptively mild tone, but with obvious authority, and the exile turned, headed back into the building, without so much as another word.

"What the…?" Chaz's shock was palpable.

Well, it was a good thing he wasn't going to have to fight the guy because right then he looked like she could have knocked him over with a feather.

"He won't be bothering you. Any of you. Ever again. Elise, always a pleasure." Kai's smile for her was wide. Stunning. And she had to admit, she felt the tiniest bit weak in the knees.

Even after all this time.

With that he spun on his heel, and she followed his powerful, regal stride as far as she could until the closing of the center's darkly tinted doors barred her view, and Chaz's insistent tugging on her arm pulled her attention back to him.

"Lise?! What in the world?! You wanna tell me who the heck that Jason Momoa-looking dude was? He's a defender, right? I saw those bright blue eyes like the ones who deal with the public always have. Lise? How do you even know him?"

"Just a friend I met a while ago. That's all. Long story."

"I'll bet. Well, yuh know I got all day, so spill it. Details baby girl. I cannot believe you... How could you keep something like this from me…?"

Shaking her head with a smile as Chaz grasped her arm to get her moving, even as he continued talking, she took a last look back at the center entrance.

She wondered if any of the people she'd tried to persuade to come to the shelter would do so, instead of returning to get implanted. She dared to hope they would.

Her last thought was to wonder about what was going on behind those heavily fortified doors, right then. And thinking…

Yes, that must have been a sight to see, indeed.

Chapter 15

Matthew 6:14
For if ye forgive men their trespasses, your heavenly
Father will also forgive you...

"Okay, so this place must have been a sight to see back in the day, huh? Nothing like it existed anywhere else in the world at that time. Although, I have to say, suddenly I feel right at home."

"Really? How so?"

"I know we're in the heart of Rome, at the Colosseum, but I swear, this aqueduct simulation looks almost exactly like the stone bath in the spa at the gym where I work. Guess this must be the inspiration for the model they used."

"Wait… You go to a gym?"

Elise took in Archie's poster child 'dad bod' for the hundredth time and resisted the urge to tell him to either change his AI exercise partner, or fire his personal trainer.

Immediately.

"What?" He gave her that adorable, perplexed

look of his.

"Oh, nothing. It's nothing, really." She reached out and touched his arm. "I just didn't peg you for the uh…gym-ing type, that's all."

"Well, there you go. There's a whole lot you don't know about me yet."

"I realize that." Curious about her fellow dream-trekker she decided to use this opportunity to advance her favorite pastime of late, namely trying to figure out just who the heck he was in real life. "So, how about we change that?"

"Hey, you show me yours. I'll show you mine." He wiggled his eyebrows.

"Oh-ho-ho, again with the jokes," she laughed. "Okay, I'll bite. What do you wanna know?" She let some eager tourists pass by, then pulled him over to a quiet corner of the steamy bathing chamber to get them away from the foot traffic for a bit. "Ask me anything."

"Anything?"

"Any-Thing." She gave him her most sincere 'I'm an open book' nod.

"Okay… So, I'm curious…how old were you when you first made love?"

"Anything but that!" She gasped. "I don't think I know you well enough to answer that question. Really? No warning? You just go straight to it, don't you?"

He shrugged with a smile.

"What? Is there like a guy's handbook somewhere that says you need to ask every woman you meet that question? Next please." She giggled as she felt her face heating up.

"You see, I knew you weren't serious about us getting to know each other."

"No, I am. I am." She took a deep breath. "All right, all right," looked down at the unusual and very ancient stonework under their feet. "I…uh…I haven't gotten that close to any guy yet. Okay, there. I said it. My secret is out."

"And completely safe with me…" He eyed her. "Really?" He looked surprised, bemused…and pleased? All at once.

"Yep. I'm as clueless about men and what they're like in bed as you can get. What? You mean there's not like a 'Twenty-eight-year-old virgin! Right here!' sign, stamped across my forehead in this dimension?"

He shook his head slowly on a wry laugh.

"Huh…well that's weird. Go figure." She gave him a quirky grin.

She didn't think she was ready to open up about what her tragically interrupted relationship with Danny had done to dampen her dating life up to that point. So, to interrupt whatever he might have been about to say as a follow up to her very private confession, "Okay, my turn," she rushed right into her first query for him. "Are you married?"

"No, of course not." His brows shot up.

She took it as a good sign he looked genuinely shocked at the question. Definitely not the look, or reaction of a liar. Or a player. "And tell me… What do you do, your job I mean, in the real world?"

"Hey! That's two. It was supposed to be my turn."

"Yeah, yeah, so sue me. Answer the question."

She grinned.

"I thought you'd have figured that out by now." He smiled back. "I'm in government."

"Well, duh…that wasn't vague at all."

He chuckled. "What can I say, there's not that much to tell… I'm–"

"Hey! Watch it!" She pulled him towards her and a bit to the side, as a big guy using his wrist cam while walking backwards nearly barreled into them. "Geez, some people can be so careless. And so rude!" she said loudly when the guy just glanced over his shoulder and didn't even offer an apology.

"Okay, my turn again. So, no lovers, huh? First kiss then? What was that like?" Archie already had his next question at the ready.

"OMG! Seriously?" She gave him a playful slap on the arm. "Who knew you had such a one-track mind. Okay, let's see… That's actually an easy one. Milton Frederick. I was fifteen and it was awful. All five seconds of it. I think. I barely knew him. It was like some kind of ninja sneak attack. I was leaving a friend's party and he just kind of rolled up on me out of nowhere, and before I knew it, he'd spun me around and had his tongue down my throat."

"Okay, so that's both disgusting and disturbing."

"You have no idea."

"What'd you do?"

"I was so stunned I just kind of stood there. Then he grinned at me like he'd just won a lottery without paying for the ticket and walked away."

"A predator in training." He frowned.

"Yep, that's what I figured. Later, when the shock wore off, I remember being really grateful that all he'd managed to do was kiss me."

"Yeah, there's no telling with a guy like that. He could have attacked you." His expression turned angry.

"Well, yeah, but that's not it. My best friends in the whole world were two tall, brawny teenage boys, and they were both right nearby and saw the whole thing. If he'd even so much as *tried* to hurt me, they would have for sure gone to juvie for kicking his butt and putting him in the hospital, or worse. For their sakes, thank God he wasn't a complete moron with a death wish."

"They still around?"

"One of them, yeah." She felt that familiar wave of sadness wash over her.

"Okay, that's good. Not that one's gone," he added in a rush, "I meant it's good to know you still have at least one of them to watch your back like that. That's a real blessing. What happened to the other one?"

"He was in a bad accident… Years ago… He passed away."

"I'm so sorry. That must have been devastating for you."

"Yeah…it was. He was…my lifeline. In every way and at a time I desperately needed one. My anchor. In a sea of emptiness."

"Oh wow… How do you mean?"

"I grew up with a father who cherished his *other* daughter, and a mother who adored her son."

"And you?"

"Oh, I'm sure they tried the best they knew how. But for me, it just always felt like they tolerated me when they could, and then controlled, dictated and ultimately stifled all that I was…when they couldn't. I lost so much of myself in those years. That I don't think I could ever get back. Conforming continuously to the standard of behavior they insisted on. All the time. It was soul crushing. Exhausting. But Danny, bless his heart, he made it all bearable.

"And then one day, he was gone. Way too soon.

"Took me a long time to be comfortable with the woman I became because of everything I've endured. It's hard to stand in your own power, when you've been repeatedly told…and shown…you don't have any. Know what I mean? Sometimes I'm still not sure who I really am. Inside."

"Oh…Lise… I'm so sorry."

"It's fine. It was a long time ago." She dismissed it all with a wave of her hand. Automatically, and just like she always did.

Except…

She'd convinced herself that at the grand old age of twenty-eight she'd gotten over it. So, it was more than a bit unsettling for her to see that the look of concern, even pity, on his face said different.

He placed a gentle hand on her arm. "Your turn again."

"Right." She shook off old memories and savored the pleasant feeling his touch evoked instead, as she considered what to ask him next. "So, what about *your* first kiss? Uh… How old were you? Just out of kindergarten? I presume."

"Ha. Ha. Very funny. Actually, I was like seventeen. Yeah, I think that's how old I was."

"Seriously? You're kidding, right?"

"What? I was really shy as a teenager. Took me quite a while to get up the nerve to ask a girl I liked to go out with me, and even longer to kiss her."

"Yeah, I can believe that. And now?" She pulled his gaze to hers with what she hoped was an encouraging brush of her fingers against his arm.

"What? What about now?" Instead, he looked and sounded nervous.

"Uh… Are you seeing, or interested in anyone?"

"Are you?"

"No, not at the moment." Unbidden an image of an incredibly handsome face with messy-sexy hair popped into her head. "Not exactly." She thrust him from her mind.

"So, which is it? Not at the moment, or not exactly?" Now he looked amused.

"No. Not at all. There was someone. Someone I thought I could really care about, but I think I misjudged him and now…"

"And now?"

"Now, I think that ship has sailed." She sighed. "But hey, no fair. I asked you first. Is there anyone special in your life right now?"

"Same story," he shrugged. "I…uh, think I may have gone down a wrong road with someone too. Zigged when I should have zagged." He shook his head on a dry chuckle.

"Yeah, strange how that can happen, huh?"

"Yeah…the strangest."

He had the sweetest look on his face just then. She smiled, took a slow step forward, towards him, and then another. His brown gaze locked into hers…and he leaned in, ever so slightly.

She leaned as well…set her expression to willing, hoping he'd take her hint…and waited…

Right up until he blinked a couple of times and abruptly pulled back.

"Uh…where are Raphie and Kai? Have you seen them?" He turned from her and started looking around him, and right on cue they appeared. Coming around the corner quite close to where they were standing. "Oh, there you are."

"What's up? You guys seen enough already?" Raphie got to them first.

"Yeah. I think so. Lise?" He turned back to her.

"Oh…uh yeah. Sure," she nodded.

"Well, okay then. Next stop, the Pantheon."

"And we're walking. Let's go people. Chop, chop. Time's a wasting, and we're burning daylight. You know what they say…"

Elise gave a half laugh in response, as Kai launched into his tour director persona humor, but inside, she wanted to groan aloud in frustration.

Well, that was a complete bust.

She'd felt sure Archie was about to kiss her. So, what the heck just happened? Wasn't he getting the signals she was sending? She'd done everything but grab him by the back of the neck and plant one on him.

Yes. There was no doubt in her mind he knew exactly what she'd wanted in that special moment they'd just shared. And she knew he wanted it too. She'd seen it clear as day. In his body language as he leaned towards her, and in his eyes. She may have known next to nothing about men when it came to sex, but she knew physical attraction when she saw it, and she could bottle and sell the pheromones rolling off of him in waves just then. Especially since everything in this dream realm the angels designed had the sensation and awareness factors bumped up by what seemed like a thousand percent. She felt everything that was good about them, and the experiences they created. Keenly.

Well at least it wasn't a complete loss. They'd made good progress. Little by little over the last couple months he had opened up and given her multiple small glimpses into the man that he was. Sure, they'd just played their little 'who am I' game. But in truth, as time went by, she cared less and less about trying to find out his full name, or to interrogate him for clues about who he was in the real world. Because more and more, she saw clearly the person he was when he was with her, and that was all that mattered.

Yes, she'd learned everything she needed to know. And she was fairly certain she'd shared all that was necessary to open the door to them taking the next step in their blossoming relationship.

Now, that next move was entirely up to him.

Chapter 16

Isaiah 40:29
He giveth power to the faint; and to them that have no
might he increaseth strength...

"So, honorable members, in conclusion, I think I've shared everything necessary to raise a motion to recommit this bill. You have before you the clinical science supporting the claims I've made today regarding how the Verndari implantation could affect our children. In far different ways from the adult population. Altering their brain chemistry. Bending young impressionable minds in ways we can't yet comprehend and certainly don't have the technology to reverse.

"I've presented you with petitions from over ten million concerned citizens. Interested groups as well as parents who love their children and don't want to see them get disfigured and harmed in irreparable ways.

"I mean, just think about it for a second. There's a reason you don't let your kid go out and get a tattoo.

Right? How is this any different? From what we've seen, that mark is permanent. Even if the medical impact proves not to be as dangerous as we anticipate, you're still talking about scarring them for life.

"The defenders are pushing out a media blitz like we've never seen. Promoting all the new free stuff that everyone can access if they get implanted. I understand they've even added in several tech toys that would be really enticing to the teens they're trying to target. We're adults, we can make that kind of decision. But a twelve-year-old, with their entire life ahead of them, who can just waltz into any Verndari center and get it on a whim, may wind up regretting that choice for the rest of their lives. I just think we need to stop and really, seriously consider what that actually means in real terms and not get railroaded into this by another Verndari branded campaign.

"Take everything you have before you, weigh it and think. The science is sound. Sure, there's a possibility we're wrong about the severity of the impact. But what if we're right? Or, what if it proves to be even worse than we could possibly imagine? Think about your own children and our future generations and ask yourself, do you really want to take that chance?" He paused and looked around...

"Honorable members, thank you. I yield the floor."

Thank you, Senator Reynasis, for that impassioned and lengthy presentation." The majority leader's tone was dry as he rose to his feet. "You've certainly given us a lot to think about. This house sits in recess."

Sitting a few rows back, Finn had listened and heard every word.

Impressed with the way it turned out and heartened that it finally looked like somebody was getting through to the powers that be, maybe even better than he could have.

He'd been racking his brain for months, trying to think of all the ways to safeguard their great nation's children and ease their parents' minds and stop their sleepless nights, worrying over the barbaric branding of their young, loved ones. He was thrilled to have been a part of the top-secret committee that was finally making a real difference, culminating in that day's event.

He had looked around during the presentation, sought out the habitual sleepers, and even those goodly gentlemen and ladies remained alert throughout. They even seemed interested, or at the very least, not completely opposed to what was being shared.

He had to admit too, he'd had his reservations when he saw the members who quietly expressed an interest in joining the cause, and in forming their little informal clandestine committee. And even more surprised to see one of them in particular volunteer for the filibuster they'd just orchestrated. True he didn't know that much about the guy. A bit of a backbencher. He'd never been particularly outspoken in the chamber. In all the time he'd been in Senate, he didn't think he'd heard him make a single contribution. He was, however, quite well known for his publicly expressed concerns about the defenders. Who knew he'd have such a persuasive presence, and good command of the material, and in such a short period of time. To say nothing of the control that he exhibited all day as he stood before them and held his ground amid the sparking of jeers and protests here and there. From both sides of the aisle.

It really was surprising too, given his appearance. He certainly didn't look like he could compel the attention of the floor the way he had. Nondescript, average height, middle-aged, balding, and not in the best shape. Not surprisingly, he was one of the few unmarried members of the Senate in his age group. Not to be unkind, but the words introverted and ordinary immediately came to mind when he thought of the man.

So, big kudos to the guy for having such a strong will though.

And an even stronger bladder.

Yes, he'd certainly dispelled all stereotypes and made his mark that day.

Senator Archibald Reynasis of New Atlantis had absolutely come through for them all, and they owed him a great debt of gratitude.

Big time.

Chapter 17

Proverbs 7:18
Come, let us take our fill of love until the morning: let us solace ourselves with loves...

"**Do you even** know where you're going?"

"For the umpteenth time, we're just out for a drive Archie. Anybody ever tell you, yuh talk too much? You're really starting to get on my last nerve right now. Yuh know that? Big time!" She took her eyes off the road and glared at him.

"Watch out! Dear God! Eyes on the road, Lise!"

She looked back, "I see it!" Pulled sharply on the steering wheel and swerved around the startled bovine that had just ventured onto the roadway directly in front of them.

"What in the hell? What's with the cow?!"

"Long story."

"I'll bet. Okay…and now? Are those sheep? Look, there's a whole passel of them, straight ahead."

"And I see them. What did I just say? Will yuh shut up with the side-seat driving for just one second so I can concentrate? Please? Can you do that?"

"Sor-ry. Geez. Anyhow, I guess since you're barely clocking fifty kilometers an hour, it'll be tomorrow before we even get close enough to hit any of 'em. Is this seriously how you dream of driving? This is just crazy."

"Archie…I swear, if you call me crazy one more time. So, help me–" she said through gritted teeth.

"Not you! I said *this*. *This* is crazy. The cow. The sheep. Talking about the random animals wandering out onto the roadway. That's all."

She took her eyes off the road again, for just a second, to glare at him and gauge his sincerity. Lucky for him he passed the test.

"What is with you and the 'don't call me crazy' thing anyway?"

"Another long story, for another time."

She took a deep breath, focused her attention on the stretch ahead of them, cleared her mind of the unwanted elements of that treasured romance novel, and pictured that section of the road completely empty.

"There. See? No more sheep. Happy now?"

"Yes. Thank God."

"Yuh know, for someone who says they're pretty well-travelled, you sure are easily spooked by some livestock," she glanced over at him. "Where's your sense of adventure?"

"I left it back with my body."

"I doubt that." She let out an indelicate snort. "Tell the truth. You aren't comfortable with any of this. Here, or back in the real world, are you?"

"Maybe." He shrugged looking adorably

sheepish.

"And for goodness' sake. Will you put on your security belt already? I'm not gonna tell you again."

"Seriously? We're in the dream realm Lise. What could possibly happen?"

"Anything. And that's exactly my point. Need I remind you? You were just spooked by a cow and some sheep."

"Fine." He huffed and complied, pressing the button on his passenger side consul that encased his left shoulder and chest in energy shield protection. "I swear, anyone looking at us right now would think we're an old married couple, or something," he grumbled under his breath.

"Excuse you? Who you calling old?"

"What? What'd I say? It was nothing. I'm sorry. Just a figure of speech. That's all."

"Uh-huh," she glanced over at him again. Took in his befuddled expression and reddening face extending up to his cute balding head, and had to stifle a burst of laughter. He really was shaping up to be the sweetest guy she'd ever met. Afraid he might be offended by her expression of amusement; she settled on a quirky smile instead. After all, she wanted to tease him, and shake him out of his shell a bit more, not hurt his feelings.

"So, what's *your* dream? Your ideal picture of a good time?"

"That's a tough one. Not sure I could name just one. But what I will say is I love the way every place we visit is such a grand occasion for you. Your joy, it's really infectious. Yuh know that? Britain, Belgium, France, Rome, Venice, Switzerland.

Everywhere we've been in the last couple months has given me an entirely new perspective on international travel. Are those all places you've dreamed about visiting at one time or another?"

"Oh yeah, and then some. I've got a whole list of countries and famous tourist attractions on my bucket list. Also, you didn't hear this from me, but I'm kind of partial to romance novels, especially the ones where the heroine travels to a foreign land to meet and fall in love with her hero."

"You read that stuff?"

"I do, and probably a whole lot more than I should."

"Wow…"

"What? Don't I look the part?"

"What part is that?"

"You know…the doe-eyed optimist. Just waiting for her prince charming to come sweep her off her feet?"

"No, as a matter of fact, you strike me as more of a pragmatist."

"And you would be right. But hey, even us realists need a little trip into fantasyland every now and again. It keeps us sane on the one hand, while we keep reaching for the stars with the other."

"Hmm…" He looked like he wanted to ask her something else, but then changed his mind. "Anyway, whatever's motivating this side of you, I feel like I'm living vicariously through your eyes every time we visit some other country. I know we've been meeting under really weird circumstances, but all things considered, I've enjoyed every minute of it. Really. It's been truly inspiring for an old, jaded soul like mine. So, thank you."

"Well, I'm glad I could do that for you. But I'll bet you're not even that old, in real life." She waited, wondering if her gentle prodding would make him open up and tell her even more about himself.

"I sure feel like it sometimes. I've been to the UK, and right here in the Emerald Isle quite a few times, and I don't think I've ever stopped to admire the landscape the way you're doing right now. Not even once."

"Really? But it's so beautiful. Just look at it." She gazed out her right driver-side window at her fantasy view of the gorgeous Irish countryside lit by the afternoon sun. Just chock full of rolling hills, baby lambs ambling along over large square patches of every shade of green. Tinted with hints of yellow, orange, red, purple, blue, and brown. "How could you not fall in love with a view like that?"

"Yeah…how could I not?"

And there it was.

The move she'd been waiting on him to make, for what seemed like forever. And then some.

Glancing over at him as she sensed and heard the change in his tone. It resonated with her in a new and wonderful way. Like a vague hint of a treasured memory, she couldn't quite recall, but just knew she'd experienced, and relied upon, time and time again. No fireworks, but rather just simple, old-fashioned comfort. And wasn't that all that really mattered? All that anyone could ever need or desire?

Suddenly she was captured in his soft gaze. Welcomed and reassured. Measured. Recognized for all that she was, and yet still treasured.

And held…so warmly, in the strikingly ordinary brown eyes looking back at her, with such care and–

"Okay guys, so this looks and sounds to me like things are getting a tad personal between you two. Maybe I should step out of the car for a bit?"

"No. No…of course not." Her gaze snapped back to the road ahead. She gripped the steering wheel as she mentally tugged herself back to the moment. "That's really not necessary Kai."

"Definitely not. We're fine." Archie's voice sounded even higher than usual. He cleared his throat and chimed in beside her. "We're fine? Right?"

She gave a vigorous nod. "Yeah. Right. Absolutely. Couldn't be better. Just another great day in dreamland."

"You sure?" This from Raphael who was seated in the back beside her guardian. "Because I'm with Kai. Like, get a room already you two." He grinned.

"What?! Really Raphie? How could you say something like that? I am shocked! You're really taking this 'joking like a human' thing just way too far right now." Her clearly articulated protest joined Archie's loud incoherent one, reddening face, and near purple now, balding head.

"Okay, so you know what the solution is. Don't you?" In her rearview she saw Kai turn to Raphie.

"Aww yeah," Raphie grinned back. "High time to take this D.I.E.T. into–"

"Hy-per-drive!!!" they both exclaimed simultaneously.

"Hyperdrive? What? What'd you mean by that? Raphie?"

"You'll see."

"Wait! I'm not so sure that's such a good idea. Besides, isn't there anything else I need to know before tomorrow? Any other pointers you need to give me before I speak at the rally at the shelter?"

"No. I think we got it covered. Both you guys already know everything you need to, for whatever happens next."

"Wait! No! Woah!" She shrieked as her cute Irish rental car got instantly switched into a Ferrari Sky-Reacher and she, unceremoniously tossed into the luxurious, leather-lined back seat beside Kai. He chuckled as he helped steady her, as she nearly toppled into him with the velocity of the switch.

"Now, that's what I'm talking about," Archie's voice took on an uncharacteristic, supremely masculine rumble, very nearly echoing the roar of the Ferrari's engine, as he addressed Raphael. They bumped fists, as he settled into the driver's seat, his soft belly nearly touching the racing car's low steering wheel, and right before she felt the car's silky-smooth, but rapid shift in speed along the roadway, in immediate response to his actions.

"Wait. Raphie? Kai? Where's my bonny Eire?" Frantic, she glanced around. "I don't see my sheep, or my cows anymore. Guys? Where are we right now?"

"I'd say somewhere between Munich and Salzburg." Kai informed her.

"What?! As in Germany or Austria?" She took another long look out her window at the cars whizzing by on either side of them at jaw-dropping speeds. "You know, I don't really recall this being one of my dreams though. Kai?"

"That's because it's mine." Archie grinned at her via the car's rearview display.

"What?! You?! You've got to be kidding me. Do you even know how to drive?" She gave it a second, then didn't take it as a good sign when he didn't respond. As if her life wasn't wild enough, now she was risking possible death on the Autobahn?

She took in a deep breath, "It's okay, we're okay…" and tried to reassure herself. "So, on the bright side we're not really in any actual danger, since this is still technically just a dream. Right? Kai?" She urged him to agree with her.

"Well, yes and no. It's like I told you, it's kinda complicated, and it is the mind that makes everything real, remember?" He shrugged.

"What? So, we're back to the *Matrix* parallel again? Is that it, Morpheus? Are you saying I could have a heart attack in here, for real?! Okay, stop this car. Right now, Archie! I need to get out and get some air." She fanned herself, feeling like she was about to start hyperventilating.

Kai's expression was solemn, and she felt her heart leap into her throat…at least until he started laughing.

"Come on now, Lise, I'm just playing with you. You should see the look on your face right now."

"Seriously?! Oh, so you've got jokes, at a time like this? Is that it?"

"What's the matter Lise? Where's *your* sense of adventure?" Archie yelled over the roar of the car's engine. "Hey," he shrugged, "you drive your way. Now…we *fly* mine. Buckle up buttercup!"

His shout of triumph mingled with her scream of excitement mixed with terror, and both angels' roars of laughter as they accelerated even faster along the superhighway, and took off into the air, rocketing into the stratosphere at hyper speed.

Chapter 18

Deuteronomy 28:7
The LORD shall cause thine enemies that rise up against
thee to be smitten before thy face: they shall come out
against thee one way, and flee before thee seven ways...

"Okay, so you can just forget about me riding in some super-fast sports car at hyper speed ever again Kai. Because this right here…is the only way to travel."

Elise sighed in sheer contentment as she leaned back in her super comfy padded chair in the luxury dining car of the world's fastest bullet train, travelling from Hong Kong to Beijing.

Just like in the millionaire businessman romance she'd read a while back, there she was, zipping along at over six hundred kilometers an hour. Thanks to the long-range, high-tech forcefield that was keeping them suspended high above even the country's tallest skyscrapers, she had nearly no sensation of the speed at which they were travelling at all. Except of course for the odd curve in the electronic track, which could be a bit harrowing she had to admit. Especially if you chanced to look out the windows as the sleek, ultra-modern carriage tilted ever so slightly to compensate for the change in its center of gravity, and you got a really good view of exactly how fast it was going, relative to the land and water features below.

Just like the representation in the novel, this particular midair train trip boasted a full-service experience, for those who wanted some of the elevation ordinarily only attributed to an airplane ride, but with way more amenities. The fully self-contained cabins had transparent upper decks that afforded the inhabitant extraordinary panoramic views of the surrounding sky, and breathtaking glimpses of the Great Wall. It sported a swimming car, a gym, an absolutely rockin' dance club, and an assortment of highly personalized entertainment, depending on your particular taste.

In fact, the only thing missing right then was the twenty-ounce Porterhouse steak, and a flute of precisely chilled Dom Pérignon vintage champagne, just like the heroine enjoyed in the very first chapter of the book she'd read. And she would have asked for it too, if she could ever stomach eating that much meat in one sitting, or if she'd ever acquired a taste for alcohol.

Unless…

"Wait…this isn't the train from that Agatha Christie novel I started reading last week, is it? *Murder on the Orient Express*? Because that would definitely not be my idea of a good time." She reached across the table between them and touched his hand when he didn't immediately respond.

"Kai?"

"Really?" His blank face spoke volumes.

"Hey, how would I know. This D.I.E.T. is your brainchild, not mine."

"But from your fantasy bucket list. Remember? I just amped it up for you. Besides which, this is an ultramodern airborne train, Lise." His voice took on that mild, 'listen up, here's where I teach you some stuff,' tone. "The Orient Express book was set in 1934. You'd be hearing the chug-a-chug-chug of the coal engine propelling it along the iron tracks, as you follow the mile-long smoke trail through your window. Plus, in all the time since you first got to know me, when have you ever been in any real danger in these otherworldly dimensions, huh?"

"Uh…have you even met me? Only every other night in the dang void. It's not like going through ceilings to avoid a tidal wave is just a regular Sunday for me."

"Okay…so that's also about spiritual growth and–"

"Hullo? Should I also remind you about needy fashion lady, freak boy's crotch in my face, and then that awful collapsing room thing. It felt like that *Inception* movie, only straight outta hell."

"Huh?"

"You know, the movie with the crazy twisty buildings turning in on each other. It kinda reminded me of that, once they all left and it got really scary and dark."

"Oh, yeah. I hadn't noticed the parallel before, but now you mention it, I see what you mean."

"Exactly. So how about that?"

"Hey, chalk it up to personal growth. Plus, that one doesn't really count. *YOU* did that to you. You said so yourself, remember?"

"Only too well. But thanks for the timely and uncomfortable reminder I'm my own worst enemy."

"And schizophrenic, apparently." He barked out a laugh.

"Really?" It was her turn to make the face.

"What? Come on… Even you have to admit, that was pretty funny."

"Uh-uh. No-ooo," she gave a vigorous shake of her head, "No I do not, actually."

"Okay, be like that. But if it was about Chaz, you would have been laughing your head off just then. I'm just saying."

She pictured the scenario, and a little giggle erupted from her throat.

"Okay, so maybe that reference was slightly funny, in the circumstances."

"Uh-huh…" He smiled at her as she grinned. "Oh, and by the way, scary? Yes. Absolutely. But dangerously life-threatening? No. Never. Not one single time."

"And I would know that, how exactly?"

"The number of hairs on your head, remember?"

"Oh, yeah right." A wave of comfort flooded her entire being at that recollection.

"Wins every argument. Every time."

"You're telling me. I've gotta remember to use that one myself sometime. I'm running out of positive   'this-is-all-for-the-best-you'll-see' affirmations to say to the senator every time I have to rescue him from some kind of killer dessert." She shook her head. "Peach cobbler. Just last week. Did you know that?"

"Yeah, that was wild. Haven't seen that many exiles gang up on one of you like that in a while."

"Really? I only saw the aftermath from when I pulled him out. Like always. How many were there?"

"Initially? A couple million, at least."

"What?!" She felt her heart plummet. Right before it started racing with her mingled shock and horror.

"Oh, I'm so sorry, Lise. I didn't mean to scare you like that." He reached out and touched her hand lending her a good portion of his feel-good comfort and fortifying joy. She soaked it in and felt the anxiety immediately recede, but not her curiosity over his revelation.

"Oh, dear God…what does that even look like?"

"Like an ocean of pure evil. Each one of them deceptively indistinct, like a random drop of water. But together – an endless sea of well-orchestrated deception and malice."

"Wow… I can't even conceive of it."

"No. You can't. And it's better that way. Trust me."

"I believe you." He'd get no argument from her on that score. "But…would the senator… Did he see them?"

"No. Michael made sure of that."

"Who?"

"Archangel Michael?"

"Oh, of course. Silly me. So, he's really out there? Fighting the exiles for us?"

"Like you wouldn't believe. He's everywhere at

once, wielding the power of the Three in One against evil. Leading the warring angels as they conquer the forces of darkness. In every time and in every dimension."

"Wow… That must be something to see."

"Yeah, it is."

"And the senator didn't even know the half of it. That's amazing. Poor guy. He was so spooked by whatever he *did* see. Can't even imagine how he would have reacted if he only knew about what he *didn't* see."

"And the beauty of it is that he'll never know it. Neither of you will. Well, this side of heaven anyway. It's like what happened at that Verndari implantation center the day you got those people to decide against taking the mark. You saw me, but what you didn't see was Michael, and a battalion of his best warriors standing toe to toe against just as many exiles."

"Wow." Her brain teemed with images of what such a spiritual battle must have looked like until–

"Yeah, it was glorious! Imagine a sea of black. Michael draws his sword of pure light rallying the brothers and then one by one their light just starts catching, spreading and growing, one to the other, until there's no darkness left. Anywhere. And everywhere for as far as you can see there's not an exile in sight. Nothing but the consuming and purifying holy light of the blessed Three in One."

She realized that her puny imagination hadn't even come close to the picture he'd just painted for her.

"Michael and God's loyal army vanquished

them all, while they were operating in a dimension you wouldn't even be able to perceive. Scores of them at a time with every flash of their awesome God-given light."

"Well, all except for the one who threatened me, right?"

"No, him too."

"But how? I saw him walk back into the center."

"From your perspective and in your limited linear view of time that's what it would have looked like. The best I can describe it for you to understand is to say that you saw an echo of what he was, but in reality, he was already cosmic dust. From the dawn of time. From the day our Lord gave his life for you on that torturous cross. And from the very moment he threatened you."

"So, when you told him he was done?"

"He was. Literally. Three words Lise – It. Is. Finished. Never forget it."

"Incredible…" she shook her head in wonder. Her mind completely blown, she tried to wrestle with the concepts he was introducing to her of how all such things could exist and be true, all at once.

"Anyway, enough of that. Don't want you to hurt that pretty little head. You've got enough to think about as it is. As in, back to the business at hand. It's time for you to make a decision young lady."

"I know. Believe me I know." She nodded and sat up straighter in her seat. "I've done nothing but obsess over this for the last two months at least. You know that."

He nodded. "So, the moment of truth has

arrived. Don't you want to know who Archie is? It's time. You're the only one who can make this decision you know. And it has to be made. Search your heart. And take comfort in the fact that there are no wrong answers. Whatever you do."

"All things work together?"

He nodded; his expression solemn. "Is there anything I can do to help?"

"Tell me what to do? Who to pick?"

"Allow me to rephrase – Is there anything I can do for you, *other* than that?"

"Arrrggg!" She put her forehead on the table and fake screamed for a couple seconds.

Raising her head again she flicked her fingers through her bangs and took in a deep breath.

"Hi there. Welcome back." Kai grinned at her.

"Oh, you joke, but this is likely the biggest decision of my life we're talking about. And the choice I make, will alter the course of it. Forever. For better. Or worse, God forbid. I have to choose between the two of them, and they couldn't be more different."

She paused, hoping to hear any useful insights from him.

"What? Don't you have any tidbits of Godly wisdom for me right now?"

"None that you don't already know."

"Dang! Couldn't I just have some more time?"

"You could, but do you really want to delay any more?"

She paused to contemplate his words.

"Think about it. Don't you want to look back at this moment in your life and know that you spent every second you could with the person you love? Rather than, regretting that you hesitated, and dragged your feet, for whatever reason?"

"Okay, I hear that. So, hear me out. I did the proverbial pros and cons list, right? First, let's consider the obvious. The ever so tall and handsome senator is *really* easy on the eyes. I mean he is hot! Kinda like you, rockin' that sexy Jason Momoa look and all. Well…if you weren't working for the Lord, of course. But still…wow." She licked her lips. "Oh, sorry." She winced, wondering if she'd got a bit too inappropriate. "No offence."

"None taken." He shook his head with a smile.

"Okay cool. Where was I…oh, yeah, whereas Archie…mmm…not so much. I mean when I first met him all I could think was how awkward and odd he was. But now…now when I look at him, I just see him. The sweet, warm, and wonderful person he is on the inside. Know what I mean? He's just so sincere and humble as can be, while the other guy, well…he doesn't think so, but his confidence borders on arrogance, I think. He's rich though. Did you see that donation he made to the shelter? I mean he just dropped ten mil, just like it was nothing. I seriously doubt Archie has that kind of cheddar. Oh, no…and now I'm sounding like a gold-digger. Okay, so scratch the money argument because Archie is kind, and thoughtful, attentive, and considerate, and that's worth far more than money, every time. And he's smart. Of course, the senator, well, he's just over-the-top brilliant. Which makes me think, given his tendency towards arrogance, how long will it be before Mr. Condescending pays me a visit.

"Now take Archie… Do I have his respect? All day long. But him? I'm not so sure, especially after what he said to me that first night. Plus, I hear he's a favorite in the Senate, so he probably has aspirations for the presidency. And you know what they say about what powerful men want? Uh-huh, more power. Which reminds me…our current leader of the supposedly free world." She lowered her voice and leaned in a bit closer across the table separating them. "That levitating thing he did on inauguration day a couple years ago, and saying he's the messiah? Some people dismissed it, saying it was just special effects and a figure of speech because he's in power now. A big show for his supporters. Whereas in the Underground…" she shrugged. "So, is it true? Is he Antichrist? Shouldn't we be helping get the word out about that?"

"All in His good time, Lise…" His expression was solemn. "There is war within the ranks of evil. The father of lies is under constant siege, from all sides. His supporters jostle for power they do not even possess."

"Wow…that's why the void is in so much turmoil, I'll bet."

"In different ways, together, we will distract, use the ensuing confusion and chaos to our advantage to protect and defend our own. In the meantime, just do what you've been doing. Encouraging as many as you can to see the light, and staying vigilant and ready to go where and when the Spirit calls you."

"Okay, I'll be ready."

He nodded. "So, you were saying, about the senator?"

"Oh, yeah. I was just thinking, if he does have aspirations for high office, he might act all nice in the void when we're alone and he needs my help, but in the real world…I can't do a thing for him. How could I ever hope to measure up?"

"Okay, so question…all those things you were saying about him, do you know those to be fact, or did you just piece together a bunch of stuff you think you know based on what? Chaz's googles, a bad experience on one dinner date, and the half dozen or so other occasions you spoke for less than a half hour?"

"Dinner meeting, not a date." She was quick to correct him, but still took a moment to mull over what he'd said in her mind.

True, the longest they'd spoken was at dinner that night. Since then, the extent of their conversations had been centered around the various requirements of the ongoing shelter expansion projects. Other than in the void, they really hadn't spent any meaningful time alone.

"Oh geez… Seriously? Well, when you put it that way. Maybe I did make some snap judgements."

She groaned.

"So can't you at least tell me which of the qualities and pros and cons I'm weighing are the most pivotal?"

"The real question is…what difference do *you* think that would make?"

And just like in that old cartoon she'd seen, a lightbulb came on somewhere in her brain, and suddenly it was all crystal clear. Kai was right. It didn't matter what he, or anyone else said because she wasn't looking for guidance.

What she was really looking for was permission.

Permission to walk a path that in her mind she'd already chosen. It was her decision to make and hers alone and underpinning it all was the strong knowledge that she'd have the blessings of God no matter what she did. She didn't need anyone to rubber stamp, *or* counter her point of view. And she could make lists of supposed pros and cons until she was old and gray. No amount of procrastination would change one simple fact.

That the heart wants, what the heart wants.

"And here's where I say – it makes no difference at all…because I already know the answer." She smiled.

Kai leaned back in his seat, crossed his arms over his chest, returned her smile, and nodded.

"Yeah, you do."

Chapter 19

3 John 1:4
I have no greater joy than to hear that my children walk in truth...

"So, you say *there's something we need to experience?"*

"Yeah, you do."

"In here? Is that a good idea? I mean, is it really necessary? Couldn't you just send us back now? What about the void's creepy inhabitants?" Archie seemed to have no end of questions and looked really nervous as he looked away from Raphie and glanced around the dim, sparsely furnished room in which they were standing.

"Yeah, I'm with Archie, guys. You know how nasty they've been recently."

Feeling a bit uneasy herself, she wondered why the angels had even allowed them to be in the void at all on this occasion.

"The light will take you back pretty soon. It'll

just be for a short while. Just long enough for you to get what you came for." Raphie gave them both pointed looks. *"Don't worry. We'll be nearby. Praying distance–"*

"Is no distance at all." Both she and Archie parroted the now familiar idiom.

"Exactly." Raphie's smile was stunning. *"We've got you covered. So, just relax. And talk for a bit."*

Both he and Kai disappeared.

Get what we came for? Well, that was an odd choice of words. But as light dawned, Elise prepared to seize the opening the Archangel offered.

"So," both she and Archie said at the same time.

"Ladies first." He smiled.

"Okay. Look, Archie, I'm actually glad we got this chance to talk alone. I don't think I've said it yet, and I just wanted to tell you how much I appreciate all you've done throughout the time we've been working together like this."

"Think nothing of it. Besides, I could never have done it without you... Well...and the angels, of course."

"Yeah, of course. But you shouldn't sell yourself short. I know we've all got our insecurities, but I've gotten to know you pretty well over these months since Raphie and Kai got us working together, and I want you to know, I think you're wonderful...just the way you are. You're smart, warm, and kind. So attentive and generous. Oh, and funny! And so thoughtful all the time. The way you're always thinking up ways to help those parents who don't want their children implanted. It's truly inspiring.

The very best compliment I think I could ever give you is that since I got to know you, you've made me wanna be better...just so I could be worthy of you."

"Oh, no Lise–"

"No, let me finish. I'm not sure how else to say this, so I figure straight out is best, before I lose my nerve. Oh, wow...this is harder than I thought it would be. I've grown so much since we started meeting like this. Before, I would have never dreamed of opening up the way I have to you. I guess what I'm trying to say is, I think I'm falling in love with you and uh...obviously, I'd like to know how you feel about me. I know how much you value your privacy, and you haven't said a whole lot about the earth-bound version of you yet. But please, you have to tell me. I'm just dying to know who you are. To see you. Connect with you, in real life, I mean." She reached out and grasped his clammy hand wondering if hers felt any different, nervous as she was. *"So, what do you think? Say something, please?"*

"You have no idea how amazing it is to hear you say all that...because I feel the exact same way."

"Really? You do?" She breathed a sigh of relief as he nodded.

"But...I think I should clear the air though. Come clean, before we go any further, and I think poetically, in the place where this all started."

"What? Where what started? Come clean about what?"

"Well... You see, my given name is Archibald, true...but most people...they call me Finn."

"What?" Uncertain, she took a couple steps back.

And then another…when he, and the room around them, began to change.

As she watched, the sparse furnishings in the space rapidly disappeared, to be replaced by paint tins and brushes, neatly lined up against the far wall. She felt the sticky cling of wet paint beneath her bare feet. Smelt the pungent odor of varnish assaulting her senses, even as Archie's dull, balding head got gradually covered by familiar, thick, and messy-sexy blond waves.

Enthralled, she followed his body's slow and spell-binding ascent upward, as his torso broadened, filled out in solid, sinewy lines and lifted. Instead of his habitual slumped posture, his spine straightened until he stood tall and erect on strong, muscled legs. Last, the pleasant, average-looking face became the striking, handsome, albeit blurry features she knew every bit as well as her own.

"Senator? Dear God…I can't believe it…is it really you?" She stepped forward. His head tilted down, and familiar gray eyes regarded her from at least a foot above hers.

She reached up. Touched his neatly bearded jaw to assure herself it wasn't just some wicked hallucination of the void.

"Now who's looking like a kid at Christmas?" His lips lifted in an adorable smile as he placed his warm palm over her hand and gazed down into her eyes.

"Hey, guilty as charged." She clutched at his hand with equal strength as he grasped and lowered it from his face to her side, as he moved in even closer to her. *"You could have knocked me over with*

a feather when the room, and especially you, transformed just now."

"Transformed?"

"Yeah, one minute we were in a practically empty space, then the next, we were back in the varnish emporium from hell, where we met. And you...you were Archie, but then you just kind of morphed into you. Didn't you feel the change?"

"No. I think that was probably just for your benefit. It's been the same room we met in since Raphie and Kai brought us here. And I think you've been seeing me as whoever you needed me to be all this time, I guess. From my perspective...I was always just me."

"Wow, you're blowing my mind right now."

"Oh, and speaking of which, before I forget. Check this out..."

As she watched, he lifted up about three feet off the ground, moved backward, then forward to her again.

"You did it! You finally learned how to fly. Good for you!"

"Well, not exactly flying yet, and definitely not like you. But I'm working on it."

He came back down to ground.

"So, tell me, what you saw just now, was it really that much of a change?"

"Like you wouldn't believe."

"So, are we talking cool, like 'Transformers'. Or all cute 'horrible beast turns into the prince' kinda change?"

"All of the above. So cool! And don't get me wrong, not that you were horrible as Archie, or

anything. But it was radical, for sure. So beautiful…and so powerful all at the same time."

Unable to stop herself from touching him again, she reached up, brushed a hand against his stubbled cheek as he smiled and leaned into the caress.

"So, your first name is really Archibald, huh? How did I not know that? See? This is exactly why I should have googled you like Chaz told me to, the day before our meeting at your office that day. He is gonna give me no end of crap, if I ever tell him about this." She giggled. *"You know, given a bit more time, I bet I would have figured it out for myself. Now I put it together, you both have ties to the current administration, you're both left-handed, you like the same kinds of food. You both love Christmastime with all the cold weather and the winter snow. You even support the same team. Go Yankees! Finding out about your first name was really just the icing on the cake, now I think about it. It would have sealed the deal, for sure."*

"No, none of that would have made any difference, until now." He shook his head. *"Raphie told me the first day he and I met, you wouldn't recognize me no matter what I did, or said. And when he brought us together on that beach later on, I knew it was true. You looked at me the way a complete stranger would when they meet someone they've never seen before.*

"The first couple days I even tried to say a few things I knew you couldn't help but associate with me, and it was like you didn't even hear a word I said. I'd get a completely blank look from you, plus, that little slightly sad, 'I told you so' look from

Raphie, so eventually I just accepted the way things were and tried to move forward.

"And then something miraculous happened. As time went on, I began to see what a blessing I'd been given, and instead of being uncomfortable, I was relieved. Because I realized that just like you wouldn't recognize me no matter what I did or said as Archie, in the real world, you'd made up your mind and had this opinion about who I was, and there was nothing I could do to change that either. But now, as Archie, I could be me, with you. It was like I was given this amazing gift of a clean slate. A do over. A chance to start again and get it right. With none of the baggage of our failed, aborted relationship. No preconceived notions and no misconceptions.

"In fact, this entire experience was cathartic. And not just in relation to you and me. There's something so freeing about not having to be who everyone expects you to be. To take a break from the real world. The irony of it all is that before I got back in touch with my spirituality I was hiding so much of who I was. Who I am. So, it's no wonder you didn't see me for me. It's just like you said, I think maybe sometimes I didn't even really know who I was, myself.

"Every day I play so many different roles. People have such high expectations of me. The senator for my administration and my constituents, to my family and friends I'm the provider. The one they can always come to for financial support. I'm a guidance councilor for some at-risk youths. I'm even that same kind of emotional support for some at-risk

friends."

He shook his head with a wry laugh.

*"Sure, some of those are me, but at the same time, and on some level, none of it is. It wasn't until I started getting back into the word, and going to church, things really changed. Starting to see who I really am, in Christ, it just revealed so clearly to me I could just **be** me. And that it's okay to fail, to make a mistake. Because I'm not perfect, and sometimes I get it wrong, and I don't have it all together. And yuh know what? That's okay because bless God, He is perfect and He never gets it wrong. Ever. Who knew that being hidden in Him could make you so strong and comfortable with being seen by the world?"*

"I know, right? It's such a blessing. I wish more people knew about it and believed."

"So anyway, of course, at that point, I got to where I def didn't want you to know it was me. So, I'd get an anxious moment or two, whenever I inadvertently said something, I thought you might recognize. Like I'm pretty sure I messed up royally and called you Ms. Sharpe at least a dozen times. But just like always, you didn't even bat an eye.

"Remember that day at the wax museum?"

"Uh-huh."

"I swear, I nearly had a heart attack when you started preaching my own multi-tasking technique to me. Telling me to ski while taking a meeting?"

"Oh right! I'd totally forgot about that. I remember thinking later that with your body-type I should have probably suggested you try a complex videogame instead."

"It's just like Raphie said, you just couldn't see

or hear the real me. Not until your heart was truly open to me again."

"Oh wow…and it makes perfect sense now."

"What does?"

"After I decided to close the door to you…to us, I vowed to open up instead to finding love with a mild-mannered Mr. Average, who'd love me like I thought I deserved. Even described to Chaz what kind of man he'd be."

"And let me guess…lo and behold. Along came me as Archie?"

"Right on cue! I think it was even that same month. There you were all middle-aged, with your cute little balding head, and your thinning hair–"

"What?"

"And that one crooked tooth on the left–"

"Stop! Don't tell me anything more. Please." He rubbed a hand through his hair.

"Oh, and I can't forget about the epic dad-bod. Oh, and your little pot belly. Yuh know…I think I might actually miss that. I kind of sunk right into it whenever we hugged." Ignoring the look of shock on his face, she continued as if he hadn't asked her to stop.

"No… Way…" His look of disbelief was priceless.

"Oh, yes way. I kid you not." She giggled.

"Unbelievable. If you only knew how long I've been working on these abs, you'd know just how much it pains me to hear you torturing me like this." He sighed and shook his head.

"God really must have a great sense of humor." She laughed.

"I'll say."

"You as Archie was as far away from YOU as I could get, and almost exactly what I envisaged running towards. Well, maybe minus the dad-bod and the crooked tooth."

"Really?"

She giggled, enjoying his reaction to her teasing to the max.

"I still can't believe I didn't realize it until now." She placed a hand on his very solid chest, right above his strongly beating heart.

"So," he clasped that hand in one of his, and brushed gentle fingers of the other across her cheek, *"you aren't disappointed that your Clark Kent turned into Superman?"*

"Superman?" She tilted her head back and eyed him. *"You? Really? Pretty full of yourself, there, aren't yuh?"*

"Okay, so that was…uh… Hell, I don't even know what that was."

He ran a hand through his hair, barked out a laugh, and kept on laughing. It was rich and real. Filled the space in her head…and in her soul.

All over again. And like never before.

"Don't even know why I said that. The analogy I guess…just seemed like a good idea, right up until the words were actually out of my mouth."

"I'd have thought Thor maybe…given our history, but Superman?"

"I know, right?"

"Well, don't beat yourself up, Senator," she dropped the voice in her head to its sultry best. *"I can't tell you the number of times I've had something*

slip out of my mouth that I just wanted to suck right back on in there. Remember?" She grinned and winked as his eyes widened.

"Oh-no-no-no... you did not just say that. In here?" She heard his low growl echo around her head in a whole new way.

"Oh really? Because I believe I just kinda did."

With a rich chuckle, he pulled her into a close embrace…that felt like forever.

"So, no more pretending we aren't crazy about each other?" His eyes shined brighter than she'd ever seen them in the void. His voice in her head, was solemn and low, stoking the fire in her heart.

"Hey, what'd I say about calling me crazy?"

His eyes widened.

"Gotcha!" She grinned. *"You are too easy. I'm just messing with yuh."*

She pulled back a bit to gaze up at him, her heart expanding in impossible joy. *"No more games. No more teasing, and definitely no more pretending."*

"You make my heart smile, whenever you smile…yuh know that?" He pulled her in even closer. And held her all the tighter. *"And I've adored you… from the very instant you took my hand and pulled me right out of this wretched void on that fateful day."*

His head lowered…

Finally…

She closed her eyes. Let her lips part on a small sigh…as she tiptoed up, and leaned in–

Snap!

–And then tumbled.

"Son of a gut-buster! Kai?! Really?!" she yelled

as he beamed, caught and steadied her.

"Well, hi there."

"You couldn't wait for just like One. More. Minute? Darn it!" She slapped at his arm and hands to get him to release his hold on her. Much to his amusement, by the looks of it.

"Why? Whatever for?" His left brow lifted in mischievous question.

"Ooo…! Don't you dare give me that innocent look. You did that on purpose. I cannot believe you. Just when we were finally about to–"

"To what? Kiss?"

"Uh… duh?!"

"In the void?"

"Uh…yeah."

He shook his head with a smile.

"What? Don't just stand there shaking your head at me. What's wrong with that? God knows we do everything else in there. Speaking of which…wait…is that a cloud?" She gaped as the fluffy white form floated by. "Where are we right now?"

She looked around and didn't recognize her surroundings. She had an awesome view of an ultra-modern looking city though. Shining and shimmering silver, sleek structures peaked out at her here and there against a bright blue sky, and from amongst the clouds.

"Atop the tallest building in Abu Dabi's floating city. Completely surrounded by a solar powered energy shield and life-support system. Quite a view, huh?"

"Awesome. Beautiful. Breathtaking." She

looked left, then right. "Now answer the question!" She glared at him to get him back on topic.

"Really? That's all I get for item number twenty-eight on your bucket list? Okay, wow. Not unexpected. But still…wow."

"Oh, don't give me that. And don't even get me started on the other bone I need to pick with you."

"Another bone? Now what could that be?"

"You knew it was him and you didn't tell me? All this time. Sure, I know in the grand scheme of things I had to make that decision on my own, for my ultimate benefit, but yuh could have given me a hint. Oh, don't look at me like that. All wise and angelic. And now…now that I made my choice, and it's all said and done, you just up and snatch me away, at the worst possible time?"

"The best time, actually. In fact, the perfect time. Bless God. Trust me. Let's see… How would Chaz put it? Oh yeah…I just did you a really big solid baby-girl. We're talking huge."

"Are you being serious right now? How? How in heaven's name, was pulling me out of the arms of the man I love possibly a favor?"

"So, picture this – when you're in the void, your saved soul shines like a beacon. Like fireworks on the fourth of July and New Year's combined."

"Oh…kay…"

"So, imagine two. Entwined. Saved souls. AND they're in love. With Almighty God and each other?"

She drew in a sharp breath, as light dawned with the vivid image he was painting in her mind.

"Exactly. You getting the picture now? We're talking a nuclear light show. Attracting every lost soul and legion-cursed exile within a parsec directly to your precise location in like a nano-second.”

“Uh…really?”

“Yes. Really. Besides which, remember how fuzzy, indistinct, and numb everything that should be good feels in the void?”

“Uh, yeah.”

“Well… what would you prefer? That–?”

She got a flash of the dull sensation and lackluster experience of a kiss between her and Finn. Pleasant enough, sure, but definitely not award-winning.

“Or…you could maybe get your little butt up outta that bed you’re in right now. Get dressed. And go get your man, and… get this…instead…”

This time the intense feeling, in just a couple flashes, had her gasping for every breath as the meeting of their lips. Once. Twice. Caused a tingling and near explosion of sensation in her head, chest, her gut, and then lower…

Stunned, she was rendered speechless.

“Yeah. That’s what I thought you’d say. Oh…and you’re welcome, by the way.”

His rich, joyous laughter, and overwhelming love, was the last thing she heard and felt, echoing in her head, heart, and across all of heaven she liked to imagine.

Right before…

And after–

–he flicked her. Right on the bridge of her nose.

Chapter 20

Ephesians 2:14
For He is our peace, who hath made both one, and hath
broken down the middle wall of partition between us...

"Hi! Good morning, Gretchen." Elise alternately flicked, then pinched some color into her cheeks as she rushed up to the assistant's desk.

The young woman's mouth opened, she stared at her, her eyes wide.

"Gosh, you look so pretty today. Has anybody told you that yet? Look, I know you haven't seen me in a while," she ran nervous fingers through her bangs, "plus, I don't have an appointment, but can I see him, for just a few minutes. Please. It's important. I just deed to–"

Finn's office door whizzed open and he rushed out, wrestling with his jacket half on and half off.

"Gretch! I'll be back. I–"

He skidded to a stop as he noticed her.

Took her in from head to toe. Slowly.

Feeling strangely lightheaded under the heat of his penetrating gaze. She reached up. Tucked a strand of her hair behind her ear. Fixed the strap of his dress.

His… Red… Dress.

He shrugged all the way into his jacket and then took the three long, powerful strides that got him to where she was standing.

"Hey…"

His smile started her heart racing.

"Hey, yourself," she smiled back. "Oh wow, your hair," she raised a hand, fingered a few long, wavy strands, tucked them behind his ear. Enjoyed the feel of their softness, and his entirely new look, maybe a bit too much. She curled her fingers into a fist at her side, to stop herself from plunging them in, right to his scalp.

Eat your heart out, Thor… And Superman…

"Wow, you look amazing…so good… I mean, uh, you were right. What you said that first day. Your hair…that length. It really suits you."

"Yeah? You think so? Thanks. I'm glad you like it. Wait…didn't you see it last–" he glanced over at Gretchen who was intently listening to every word they were saying, "the uh…last time I saw you?"

"Oh, no…it looked the way it was before…to me."

"Oh, okay, and come to think of it, we haven't actually seen each other…uh…here I mean, in a while. Have we? I've been growing it out. Figured it's time I start being true to who I am. All things considered. Administration be damned. Heck, let them fire me. For what? A grooming infraction? I'd like to see them try. Either way, as long as I'm good in the Lord, everything else can go hang. Am I right?" He gave a dry chuckle.

"Amen," she nodded as she echoed his faith admission, agreeing with his entire assessment completely.

And loving the fact that he sounded just as nervous in the moment, as she felt.

"So, I take it we're okay now, Ms. Sharpe?" The left side of his mouth quirked upward as he met her gaze.

"Oh, we're way better than okay. We are great, Senator. We are…amazing. Except you should call me El…Finn."

"Mmm…I like the sound of that. Say it again…El."

"What? Finn?"

"Mm-hmm…I like the way you say my name." The tone of his voice held just the right amount of velvet and gravel.

"So, Finn…" she nearly giggled like an ingénue, "where were you off to, in such a hurry, on this fine morning?"

"I was actually just on my way out to the shelter to see you."

"You were?"

"Yeah. I was. Would have come by sooner too. As soon as I woke up, actually. Except I had a meeting I couldn't get out of."

"Me too."

She smiled. Looked up into hooded deep gray as he ran a warm palm down her bare arm to her hand. He clasped it.

"Gretch? Hold my calls, will you?"

"Sure Mr. B. Consider them held."

"Thanks Gretchen." Elise shared a brief grin with her then turned back to Finn as with his gentle but urgent tug on their entwined hands, he led her across the sleek floor, and into the privacy of his office.

The door had barely slid closed before he had her firmly pressed against it. She opened her hand. Dropped her bag. Moved that hand to his hair, slid her fingers in, and let her eyelids flutter down, as his lips descended to hers.

And clung.

He kissed her slowly at first, then with more urgency as she caught his fire. He delved deep, devoured her mouth, with eager intent, then slowed again, lingering in the best way. As though he knew just exactly what pace she needed…so she could savor, every moment of the delicious and decadent taste and feel of him. A willing participant, she hung on for every slow, hot, sweet and delicious twist and turn of their consuming ride.

He dragged his mouth away. Pulled back a fraction, dislodging her grip on his hair, even as she followed.

"I'm sorry, I should have asked," his voice was a deep, gravelly rumble. His eyes searched hers, even as his fingers continued their now familiar and distracting play along the base of her neck. "El?"

"What?" She struggled to follow what he was saying over the steady thrum of her body's call to kiss him again.

"I didn't ask… Is this… okay? If I kiss you like this?" His gaze roamed her face. "Everywhere…" he murmured. "I mean, I didn't mean to jump you. It's just after this morning, as soon as we woke up, I couldn't wait to–"

"To finish the kiss, we almost started?" Her voice came out breathy as she let her lips open on a sigh, as she leaned forward.

"Mm-hmm," he nodded once, and her parted lips landed on his chin. The only bit of him she could reach just then. The reward was an immediate jolt of awareness at the velvety, spiked marvel of his trim beard setting off wave after wave of tingling sensation in her lips.

"Yeah, I know…" She stretched up to whisper in his ear, "Me too," then dropped her nose to his neck. Inhaling the arousing aroma of citrus and sandalwood in the morning.

Mmm…

She reached up, regained her pleasurable finger-hold in his hair and pulled his lips to hers. Kissed him again. Deeply and with hunger. Once. Twice.

"Okay, wow…do that again." He pulled her back in for a repeat performance. Then dragged his mouth away again.

"Love that dress on you, by the way. Did I mention that?" He raked her with a thorough gaze down her entire body.

"Anybody ever tell you; you talk too darn much?" She pulled him back in for another breathless kiss.

"Yeah, you actually." He mumbled as he smiled, then nibbled on her lips.

"Oh, right… But yeah…the dress, I thought you might like to see it," she managed on a breathy purr.

"Mm-hmm… Looks even better on you than I pictured. On the day I bought it, and in every single dream I've had since. With you dressed in it." He let out a low growl. "And…when I take you…"

His gaze snapped up. Collided with hers. Intense… Compelling and addictive.

His head dropped then, as he mimicked his words, and took her mouth with real hunger. Ragged and uncontrolled. Greedy…and untamed.

"When… I take you…out. In it, I meant." He punctuated his words with kisses.

"Liar… No, you didn't."

He eyed her, a slow smile lit his gorgeous face.

"In it, out of it. Hey, after our wedding night…any of that will work just fine for me. I'm super flexible. In fact, as good as you look, I might have the dang thing framed as a memento of this moment."

His low chuckle was infectious.

Her joyous giggle filled her to bursting.

"I see now why you bought it for me to wear that night. You, dressed the way you were, and me in this. We would have been quite the eye-catching pair. A power couple bar none. Yes?"

"Well, you're half right," his voice was soft.

"Huh?"

"The pair and the couple part, for sure. Us. Together. No elucidation labels necessary though. Just you. And me. That's all I've ever cared about." He brushed gentle knuckles across her cheek and chin. "From the very minute I met you."

Touched beyond measure she tiptoed up, urged him with a look, to join her, as their lips met. And clung.

Again…
Somewhere, in the middle.

Chapter 21

Acts 2:26
Therefore did my heart rejoice, and my tongue was glad;
moreover also my flesh shall rest in hope...

"Lise, come with me. I want you to see something. Open your eyes."

Half asleep she obeyed Kai, floated over and met him.

Somewhere in the middle.

Somewhere between sleep and waking.

Somewhere between her sweetest dreams…and heaven.

She saw flashes then. Dozens of smiling faces. People playing, working. Just going about their daily lives. Like looking at a pleasant, family-oriented TV commercial of old, in a minute or two it was over and she was left with just the lingering feelings of love and contentment it evoked.

"Who were all those people?" She turned to Kai.

"I'm so glad you asked because those were

recipients of Danny's organs and their very grateful families. Heart, lungs, liver, kidneys, corneas, so many transplants were made possible because of him. I know it doesn't, could never make up for your loss. But I hope you'll get just a little comfort from knowing the spirit of his giving, that very best part of him, still lives on in each of the people who are alive and able to live a better quality of life because of him."

"Oh, wow…I had no idea. His mom never even told me. That's amazing and so gratifying to see and hear. Thank you, so much, for sharing that with me. I'll never forget it. It means the world to me."

"And one more thing…"

Out of the gathering mist a form emerged. Shifting and reforming until she was just able to make out a very familiar and beloved face.

"Danny?" She felt her heart soar.

"Hey El." His blurry countenance gathered then. Solidified, into sharp clarity. "You look so good."

He looked and sounded better than ever. Better than she could have ever imagined. He smiled that familiar smile she knew so well.

"Me? Oh, dear God… Danny you…you look amazing."

"Yeah, I hear heaven can do that for you."

He grinned.

She giggled.

Just like old times.

"I can't believe this. It's so amazing to see you again, like this."

"Well, I just wanted to tell *you* how happy I am to see you moving on and living your life so well.

I'm so proud of you. Just like you did for me with your love, in the short time we had together, you rescued Finn, yuh know that? And from that very first day you smiled at him in that mess of varnish." He chuckled.

"Oh, wow… You saw that?"

"It's amazing here. Beyond your wildest dreams. Now, I see everything, in ways you'd never imagine, and so will you, in His perfect timing.

"I never told you this, but you were my hero El. Now you're his. For real."

"You think so?"

"I know so. So go on… Be that super feminine powerhouse I know you can be. And absolutely no more living in the past. Promise me?"

She nodded, not trusting herself to speak, as she felt the press of threatening tears constrict her throat.

"And none of that crying either. What we had was amazing, but it's time for you to put away the things of the past. All of them." He reached out. Gently, he fingered the wedding ring his mom had given to her the day of his funeral. The one he'd bought for her, but never got the chance to place on her finger.

She nodded again, still feeling the mixing of tears of loss and joy intermingling, but more and more indistinct as she began to feel so very sleepy…

"Be happy El." Fighting to keep her eyes open, she heard his voice as though from a great distance, and as he started fading away.

"Remember… that in God's unique way and in His grace, I will love you…forever…"

"Forever…" she whispered as she drifted back

to sleep.

"Okay, so the suspense is killing me. I feel like I've been waiting forever for you to get off your coms. Didn't Mel tell you I needed to see you?" Chaz strolled into her office and took his habitual spot in front of her desk. "How'd the meeting yesterday with the senator go? You guys discuss anything important?" He gave her a pointed look.

"Oh, yeah, sorry. I actually meant to call you last night. It was great!" She had to stifle a little shriek of joy as she waved a hand across her air screen to minimize it. "Close." On her one-word command, her office door slid shut with a little whistle. "We had a voice call with the project manager remotely because Finn was somewhere in Europe and couldn't get his visuals up and running for some reason. We discussed the budgets and next steps for the new Chicago site. He pretty much let me carry the meeting, but he had a lot of great ideas too. I was surprised. Well, actually, no. I wasn't. He is really such a whiz with logistics and procurement planning. I mean I got hints of it early on during the first project. But since then, and today–"

"Today? You mean that was him that you spent all morning talking to again?"

"Yeah. What? We had a follow-up with a few of the pharmaceutical companies to see if they'll donate some of the meds we need. Anyway, today he was really in his element. And we just clicked. Maybe even better than before. It's like we could have practically finished each other's sentences. I mean–" she bit her lip in midsentence as she noticed Chaz's telling expression. "Uh…so anyway, things are right on track for our next six-month timeline, if you're interested."

"Uh-huh…"

"What?"

She knew that look.

"Girl, do I look like I give a crap about the Chicago site? How are things between you two? Personally." He gave her another pointed look. "Come on now. Out with it. You love him. For real. Don't you?"

She considered fibbing, then caved.

"O.M.G. Yes. Is that crazy? After everything that happened? He is just so amazing! He really is." Half afraid of how Chaz would tease and torment her, particularly since she hadn't told him about her, and the senator, and Archie, or anything that happened between them somewhere between sleep and waking. She tried not to prattle on, but wound up doing it anyway.

"I guess it's true what they say then," he shook his head.

"What's that?"

"That out of the heart, the mouth speaks. And baby-girl you are gushing."

"I know. I am, right? It's like I can't help myself." She giggled.

"Well halleluiah. Just look at you…after so long."

His voice got soft at the last, and she knew he was thinking of Danny. Just like she was.

He rose from his seat and so did she.

They met somewhere near the edge of her desk.

"Everything in its time and a time to every season under heaven. I'm so glad to see you embracing something new so well," he fingered the tiny crucifix she now had hanging from the chain around her neck. "It's a good look on you.

"Hmm… C.D.E. and now F. I think I like the sound of that." His smile warmed her down to her toes.

"You do?" She sniffed as she felt her eyes fill with sudden moisture.

"Yeah." He pulled her into one of his familiar and craveable bear hugs. "And I know Danny would too."

"Good. So do I." She grabbed his lapels with both hands and buried her face in his neck for a few moments as she soaked in his strength and warmth–

"Okay, so when are we doing lunch? Or dinner? 'Cause you know I've still gotta check this brother out."

…And right before she placed her palms flat on his strong chest and pushed him back.

"Okay, good talk! And now–"

"I know. I know. Get out of your office?"

"Exactly! I've got work to do, dude."

"Yeah. Yeah. I'm going." He headed to the door and looked back.

Then caught the kiss she blew him one-handed, as he grinned.

EPILOGUE

"So, that was jolly good! Wasn't it? All's well that ends well, ay?" Gabriel grinned.

"Yeah, yuh gotta love a happy ending like that. Hey, you still talking like a Brit, Buddy? What's up with that. Don't tell me Alcindor got you again?!" Raphael barked out a laugh.

"Please, I've still got several hundred earth years left on the last prank. As you well know. Still, I do love this accent. This is called enjoying the simple things, and I am loving the perks of the absolutely hands down best job in the entire universe. Can I have an Amen brother."

"Amen and Amen. I heard that."

"But while we're on the subject… You know you could start the ball of change rolling for me. Be the one that gets the big guy and the brothers to start calling me by my actual name again. Hmm?"

"No way. Besides, the big guy's enjoying it way too much. Maybe even more than Alcindor."

"Yes, I noticed that as well."

"Hey, what can I say. You're on your own. I don't play along and heaven's chief prankster's likely to set his sights on me next, and believe me when I tell you brother, that is not happening." He chuckled.

"Now *that*…that is cold my friend. Like when I spent some earth time in the arctic, cold."

"You should count yourself blessed and highly favored. You got off easy, if you ask me. I mean, remember what he did to Uriel last time?"

They both eyed each other and roared with laughter…just as Uriel popped in to join them.

"Oh, yeah, I remember. Now that was a good one. Even I couldn't stop laughing. I'd like to see him try that on someone like Michael though."

"Oh, so that's not happening. He knows Mike does not play. One slash of that lightning sword of his and he'll make him lose something from somewhere it won't grow back, without the Creator's say-so."

They all three, burst into laughter again and bumped fists in the middle of their little angelic circle.

"So, what brings you both here? Had a word with the big guy on next steps?"

"We did indeed and looks like I'll be reprising my role as Budbringer pretty soon in earth's future. Alongside our heavenly scholar of learning and philosophy here," he pointed in Uriel's direction. "And who better to reflect the one true light.

"So, come along, my good fellows, we have a veritable plethora of new D.I.E.T.s to design. And get ready because this next phase is going to be epic."

"So, who's up next? Lily or Melanie?" Raphael wondered.

"As always, He'll let us know in His good and perfect timing."

Gabriel slapped them both on their backs and grinned.

"And that time…is now."

They all turned…their faces alight with pure joy, and deep reverence…

As the Creator Himself…joined their heavenly little circle!

Did you catch the other books in the series?
Surrender
Transform
Delight

Love is Deborah Lamoreaux's raison d'être.

She lives to immerse her readers in a rich fantasy world where magical faraway places and unwavering fated love all come together to create a delicious, satisfying melting pot of literary distraction.

In her world love is always true, unexpected, undeniable, unconditional and of course… everlasting.

Ms. Lamoreaux only ever comes alive when she's let loose to produce her next work of romantic fiction and each and every time that you journey alongside her, within the pages of one of her creations, she escapes the confines of imagination…
So come, escape with her…

Sign up for Forget Me Not Romances newsletter and receive a special gift compiled from Forget Me Not Authors!